A Holiday Code for Love

The Code Breakers Series, Book 7

Jacki Delecki

BOOKS BY JACKI DELECKI

THE CODE BREAKERS SERIES
Regency Period Romantic Suspense
A Code of Love
A Christmas Code
A Code of the Heart
A Cantata of Love
A Wedding Code
A Code of Honor
The Code Breakers Series Set

THE IMPOSSIBLE MISSION SERIES
Contemporary Romantic Suspense
Mission: Impossible to Resist
Mission: Impossible to Surrender
Mission: Impossible to Love

THE GRAYCE WALTERS SERIES
Contemporary Romantic Suspense
An Inner Fire
Women Under Fire
Men Under Fire
Marriage Under Fire
A Marine's Christmas Wedding
The Grayce Walters Series Set

May this holiday bring hope and light into your world.

CHAPTER ONE

The Honorable Jack Bonnington gently steered his wife toward a narrow path in the woods. He had plans for a sensual detour before their meeting with Lord Cordelier Rathbourne, England's Spymaster, who had summoned them for an urgent meeting.

Jack feared he might be sent away from his bride. He'd heard that things were amiss in Dover and Jack was most likely the candidate to assess the problem since he belonged to the Dover Battlement Committee, which had been charged with fortifying Dover in the event of an invasion of Napoleon's troops stationed in Calais. He didn't want to leave Abbie. Jack swallowed the acid taste of fear at the thought of losing her. It was frightening how vital Abbie had become to him in the scant two months of their marriage. He had never before understood the power of obsession, never felt its ferocious pull until now.

"Jack, where are we going?" Abbie paused and looked up at him. Her bright eyes were the same color as her sky-blue pelisse.

Despite feasting on every luscious inch of Abbie this morning, he needed more. Alert to the meaning of his bride digging her heels into the damp path, Jack pulled Abbie into his arms. He knew how to change his stubborn wife's mind.

He brushed his lips over hers before coaxing her to open his mouth. The taste of Abbie sent his nerves humming his favorite melody.

"Don't you want to visit our 'special place' this morning?" The forester's hut deep in the woods had become Jack's favorite place since that was where Abbie had innocently seduced him prior to their marriage. One of his Christmas presents to her was to rebuild the dilapidated, one-sided wooden hut into a secret hideaway for them from his rambunctious brothers and his father who lived with them.

He and Abbie had made great use of "their special place" during their summer treks between the Bonnington and Rathbourne estates in St. John's Woods on the outskirts of London.

Never forgetting his terror when Abbie had been kidnapped, Jack daily escorted her to the Rathbourne estate. It was heavily guarded, but still…. He wasn't sure if he would ever again allow his wife to make the fifteen-minute walk with only Ford, the brawny ex-soldier, who served as her bodyguard. Her secret intelligence work put her at great risk.

"Jack, in case you haven't noticed, it is winter, and Lord Rathbourne is expecting us," Abby said, interrupting his thoughts.

"Abbie, we have time."

With the imminent arrival of relatives and friends for their Christmas house party, he would have to share Abbie with all the demands of the season before his likely departure for Dover—the rationale, as if he needed one—for this early winter morning rendezvous. He pulled her hard against him and kissed her desperately at the thought of not being able to protect her from any threat while away. The kiss heated instantly. Her tongue darted in and out to intertwine with his, deepening the sensations zooming through his body.

When Jack palmed her breasts through her pelisse, Abbie threw back her head in abandonment. The expanse of her pale tender neck was too tempting to resist. He raked his tongue up the soft column and swirled it across her sensitive earlobe, nipping it while fondling her breasts. Her nipples tightened through the heavy wool.

He tracked the patches of color moving across his wife's cheeks and the little catches in her breath while he circled her tight nipples. His wife would soon be amenable to his plans. He longed for the summer months when he could pull Abbie's gown down and taste. He hated her high-necked pelisse and dress obscuring her soft womanly flesh.

"Darling, let me take you to the hut. I want to make you happy again."

Desire softened Abbie's crystal blue eyes. "Jack, you're incorrigible. You already made me happy this morning."

Jack's body hardened at the memory of her fingers digging into his shoulders as she screamed his name. "Oh wife, how soon you forget. I made you happy two times, but I would like to make you ecstatic one more time. Round number three."

With his hands underneath her pelisse, Jack reached to unbutton the back of Abbie's dress.

"Three isn't a round number."

He could easily distract Abbie, a mathematical genius, with any discussion of numbers, even basic concepts. If he could only get her damn gown loosened.

"I can't wait, Abbie. I need you now." Jack pressed his hardness against her thigh, urgency tensing every muscle in his body, urging him to dive into Abbie's sweet heat.

Abbie shuddered, sending a rush of warm breath against

his. "I can't, Jack. I must see Lord Kendal before our meeting with Lord Rathbourne. The new missive I've been translating has raised some interesting questions."

"Kendal? Will Henrietta be there too?"

Abbie's head jerked up. "Why in heavens are you asking if his sister will be there?"

"Because you shouldn't be alone with the man. Any man."

"Lord Kendal is your best friend and is happily married, as you well know." Abbie shook her head, her blond curls bouncing against the bandeau, causing Jack to itch to run his fingers through her silky hair.

"It could ruin your reputation." Jack knew he was being ridiculous since Abbie had been working as a code breaker with Kendal for months, but that didn't stop the irrational mix of fear and jealousy to have taken control, the heat of possessiveness whipping a frenzy in his gut.

Abbie stepped out of his embrace, her chin tilted in the air. "You're worried about my reputation? Being alone with Lord Kendal is nothing. You should worry about the discovery of my work for the Intelligence Office. If I were ever revealed as working for the government, I'd be ruined."

Jack didn't care about Abbie's reputation. He feared for her safety.

"I'm very aware of your status as a spy and the danger it puts you in." Jack was a hairsbreadth away from demanding his wife stop her work. Except…how shallow a man he would be to deprive his country of one of its best analytical brains, as well as depriving the woman he loved of the work that made her happy.

"It isn't natural for a woman to be working so closely with a man." His jealousy of his best friend and the unfamiliar insecurity maddened him. He didn't recognize the man he was becoming.

When he'd met Abbie, Jack had to abandon all his predetermined concepts that women weren't capable of analytical reasoning. Abbie thrived on her work with Kendal and his sister Henrietta, deciphering cryptograms and creating false codes to baffle the French. Her independent spirit and brilliant mind, coupled with her unaffected warm nature, had captivated him. He hadn't been able to look away from Miss Abbie Lyon—to the extent he'd claimed her for his own.

"Jack Bonnington, I don't like the implications of your statement that, as a woman, I can't be trusted to work with a man without seducing him." Abbie's voice notched higher. "I believe that I've discovered a connection to the head of the French London spy ring. I need Lord Kendal to verify my conclusions."

Jack leaned over his wife, trying to use his size to intimidate her.

"I trust you. It's the men I don't trust." Jack kept up the irrational argument, despite being irritated with himself. How had this morning and his plans for carnal delight gone so badly? And why couldn't he just shut up?

"Your logic is faulty." Abbie poked her finger hard against his chest. As if her puny effort would have any effect. He lifted her hand and rained kisses on each of her fingers. Her stormy eyes filled with passion, causing Jack to care about nothing except reveling in Abbie's desire.

"What if Lord Rathbourne asked you to work with an attractive woman?"

"What?" Jack kissed Abbie's palm, enjoying her slight tremor as he rubbed her wrist against his rough morning stubble.

His "spy" assignment was to monitor the embezzling Lord Atwell. That a respected peer and head of the Dover Battlement Committee had been embezzling funds earmarked to pay for guns and cannons to defend against the French invasion still made Jack's skin crawl. Atwell, under the threat of imprisonment for his treasonous acts, replaced Lieutenant Hyde, the English military engineer who had been sending the strategic plans for protecting Dover to the French. Jack was now tasked with supervising the slimy Atwell in his forwarding of misinformation—created by Abbie— to the French on the plans for Dover's defense.

Jack snorted. "My days are spent dealing with the disgusting, overweight, and conceited Atwell. Not exactly dangerous work."

"What you are doing is important. The plan to lull the French into believing Dover Castle is not receiving special reinforcements to thwart Napoleon's invasion from the English Channel appears to be working, according to the latest round of French messages we've intercepted."

Jack was proud of his part in discovering a mole on the committee who had been conveying their building plans to the French. Now, they were using Atwell as a mole so they could discover the rest of the French spy ring operating in England.

"Taking your premise that Lord Kendal or I won't be able to control ourselves while working together, wouldn't the same argument apply to you working with an attractive woman?"

Abbie could never stop in the middle of an argument—her logical brain wouldn't allow it. She had to follow every thread to the rational deduction. And although Jack admired her abilities, he didn't like her conclusion.

"Why would I want to seduce another woman when I have you in my bed?"

"Jack Bonnington, you're trying to distract me." Abbie stomped down the path. "And this is an important meeting."

Jack followed close behind. "Your logic is faulty because you don't understand the minds of men."

Abbie threw her arms into the air. "I'm trying to understand. I know I lack your knowledge and experience of the opposite sex."

Jack didn't want Abbie to go down that wide and crooked path to his reputation as a rake.

"Ask any husband. Men don't want their wives spending time with other men." Jack appreciated how calm he sounded. "We're territorial and jealous. Let's ask Kendal if he'd like Gabby working with me every day."

"You are not going to embarrass me by asking Lord Kendal that. I can't believe you would consider…." Abbie muttered under her breath, "Of all the idiotic…" as she marched down the path, away from Jack. "Not all husbands think like you do," Abbie added over her shoulder. "Gabby spends time with her very handsome music teacher."

Jack enjoyed the sway of his wife's hips with her strident pace. Something else Abbie didn't appreciate. Despite any situation, men didn't stop admiring the form of their women. *Wait.* What had Abbie just said?

"You think Gabby's music teacher is very handsome?"

CHAPTER TWO

Regret washed over Jack as he tracked Abbie's march down the long hallway for her meeting with Kendal. Being husband to an independent wife was not an easy task. He wished he had someone with whom he could share this quandary of having a wife who was a spy. There was only Rathbourne…

Ladies of his acquaintance managed their households, dabbled in watercolors or studied music, but never courted danger. Not that he wished that life for Abbie. She'd be bored out of her brilliant mind.

The soldier/footman opened the door to Rathbourne's study. Jack didn't see himself discussing his personal life with his superior. As Head of Intelligence, Rathbourne wasn't the sort of chap who you would joke with or confide in.

Rathbourne sat behind his shiny mahogany desk, which was stacked with papers. Noting the dark circles under his superior's eyes and the teapot on his desk, it was clear that Rathbourne had worked through the night again. Kendal had shared that Rathbourne had been a fierce and relentless agent, saving many lives during the French mess when aristocrats lost their heads. Now, it seemed he never left his desk except to travel to London.

"Come in, Bonnington. Your wife is meeting with Kendal?" Rathbourne's cool and inscrutable inspection was always the same.

Jack considered raising the difficultly that his next assignment would cause by separating him from Abbie. However, he never shirked his responsibilities and for the heroic man behind the desk, Jack would do whatever he was asked.

"I'm to understand your sister Amelia and Lord Brinsley's Aunt Mabel are establishing Abbie's place in society with her first Christmas house party."

In the process of seating himself in his usual chair across from Rathbourne, Jack looked over at Rathbourne with surprise, knowing his superior wasn't in the least interested in society or parties.

"They've already taken over the estate, creating total havoc. As if the estate weren't chaotic enough with my brothers tumbling into disaster on a daily basis. Why I agreed to allow Amelia and Aunt Mabel to host a house party to support Abbie's reputation is mind-boggling." Actually it wasn't, Jack had to admit. He would do anything for Abbie.

"It was my idea."

Jack stared at Rathbourne. The man did nothing without a purpose. "Why would you care about establishing Abbie in society?"

"To protect her cover, it is important to keep up her appearance as a happily married wife taking her place in society."

"Abbie is a happily married woman." Jack paused, recalling Abbie's disappointment this morning with his ridiculous insinuations. It was hard for a man to concede that he behaved like a jackass. All the same, since meeting

Abbie, Jack had been getting a lot of practice. Once this meeting was over, he'd apologize to Abbie again.

Rathbourne's steely gaze seemed to apprehend every frustrating thought whizzing through Jack's brain. The man also had the ability to wait out any conversation, which was more than Jack could ever do. Jack was always at the ready to jump into any fray. He wasn't sure if his impulsiveness came from spending too much time with his impetuous younger brothers or if it was a family trait. When he reflected on the escapades of his siblings, there was no doubt about it—it was a family trait.

"I know how important Abbie's work is." Jack admired Abbie's ability to decipher French codes, but her work had also almost gotten her killed. And what had she said earlier about finding a connection to the French spy ring? If she had found a connection, would it put her in more danger? Jack's heart punched against his chest in aggressive jabs.

How did a husband, a protective, overbearing person like Jack, protect his wife? Jack knew taking responsibility for his family at a young age had forced him to mature in a way that none of his peers understood. Witnessing his father's despair after his wife's death had made Jack leery of caring that deeply until he met Abbie. And now, if he lost her, he wasn't sure he'd survive.

"We share something that no other peer can comprehend. Our wives, unlike all other ladies in society, are doing secret dangerous work for our country. It is not an enviable position."

Jack guffawed. "That's describing it mildly."

"Learn from your mistakes. Believe me, I've made them. Like you, I assumed responsibility for a large estate at a young age and then I started working for Intelligence. I was used to having control, having my commands followed. I had to discover the hard way that Henrietta didn't agree with my assumption that she should always follow my orders. In fact, she was fully capable of making decisions for herself."

"You'd be roasted alive if any man at our clubs knew."

"I didn't see you as man who cared about popular opinions."

"I don't. It's the danger. Abbie is oblivious to the threat."

"Isn't that what we want?"

"You want Abbie to not recognize the danger? I wake in a cold sweat remembering that French spy holding a knife to Abbie's throat."

"Our job is to protect our wives without ruffling their pride so they can use their prodigious minds to unlock codes. That is why we have so many bloody soldiers on the estate, and why they are heavily guarded when in society. It has been easier with Henrietta's confinement, however that is soon ending."

Rathbourne *did* understand. "Abbie gets mad whenever I try to warn her or instruct her. Is it the same with Hen? She was always game for adventures as a girl."

"My wife is very good at ignoring orders she doesn't agree with."

Rathbourne's revelations eased Jack's trepidations.

"I do remind her periodically that I'm the Head of Intelligence, to no effect. Not that I want anyone to know my wife doesn't always follow my direction. Not good for a man in my position." Rathbourne chuckled.

"Does it get better with time?"

"Easier?" Rathbourne ran his hand through his hair, a familiar gesture signaling his frustration. "No. @What I've accepted is that Henrietta is perfect for me. There are many men who couldn't tolerate Henrietta's independent mindset and capabilities. Though I can't imagine not having an accomplished wife who challenges me."

Abbie did challenge Jack. She had challenged him the moment they met, arguing that women had the right to a university education. Women usually flirted and praised Jack and always agreed with his opinions. Not Abbie. And he had been enthralled.

"Your assignment with Atwell is going to make things more difficult for your marriage."

"So, you are sending me to Dover." He was being sent, he assumed, to maneuver his way into the spy ring under the guise of his architectural work for the Dover Committee.

"There has been a change in plans. Ford arrived late last night to confirm that Sabine is working for the French. I've been aware of her activities. Her attachment to Atwell has confirmed my suspicions. Ford followed her to her townhouse where Luc Duval, a French émigré we know has connections to the French underground, was waiting for her."

Jack stared at Rathbourne's lips, trying to comprehend the words he was hearing.

Jack shook his head. "I don't believe it. Sabine is a dramatic, self-centered actress who could care less about politics or war. She knows nothing of espionage."

Rathbourne's silence was always unnerving. "She's a very gifted actress who ensnares high-profile peers as her lovers," he said after a long pause.

"She was my mistress."

"Exactly."

"This was before I worked for you. Nothing I've done puts me in French crosshairs."

"Think about it, Bonnington. Your best friend is Kendal, our code master, and you are privy to his work and have easy access to him. And your sister is Henrietta's closest friend and knows of her work."

"I didn't know of Kendal's or of Henrietta's work for the Crown until I started to work with you."

"When Sabine saw you were of no use, she discarded you. And I'm assuming that she received new instructions to take up with Atwell."

This was too preposterous—Sabine, a French spy. "I ended the relationship."

Rathbourne sat back in his chair and rubbed his chin. "You might think so. I'm guessing Sabine became difficult, jealous, demanding?"

Jack might not be as brilliant as his wife, but he definitely wasn't slow to the right deduction. The thought of wringing Sabine's pale neck flitted across his brain. He'd paid an exorbitant price to have her as his mistress since two other peers wanted her. The irony wasn't lost on him. She had played them all.

"I've arranged for Sabine to be invited to your house party."

"I beg your pardon. Who is to be invited to our house party?"

"Sabine. Prior to the party, you will meet up with Atwell at the club. You will pretend to have had too much to drink and drunkenly reveal that there are secret plans for Dover's fortification. A new explosive will be stored at Dover in the existing tunnels. You'll be working with Pettibone to design the storage area in the tunnels. And you'll let it slip that you have the plans and you'll be glad when they're finished since having possession of them endangers your family. Then complain about your marriage to throw him off. We need to know whether Atwell has sold us out by sharing this with Sabine."

"Atwell knows he'll go to prison if we expose his embezzling." With the mounting reality of French invasion,

Atwell wouldn't be able to hide behind his title to escape punishment.

"Do you think a man like Atwell believes he will ever be punished?"

"In his favor, he's been doing exactly as I demand." Jack leaned forward in his chair, not able to sit still, his mind racing to keep up with the trap Rathbourne was devising. "You always knew he'd look for a way to get out of the agreement."

"You said it yourself. The man is an embezzler. He can't be trusted. We don't have much time to discuss your house party. I hear my wife's voice in the hallway."

Jack jumped out his chair. "Everyone will think I've invited Sabine because I'm unhappy in my marriage." Sabine had approached Jack at a ball before he was married to Abbie, hoping to cause a scandal. Abbie had handled herself perfectly and became a favorite of society after the incident. However, having his ex-mistress in his home went too far.

"I will speak to Abbie about the importance of Sabine's presence to trap Atwell and to also ensnare Sabine."

"My wife doesn't need to be involved. We can devise another plan without Abbie." Jack paced the length of the plush Aubusson rug, trying not to lose his temper with Rathbourne and how he manipulated people's lives in his strategies. "There are other ways to trap Atwell that would not put my wife through public ridicule. I will not allow it." Jack accepted that Abbie contributed greatly to the war effort; still, this request went beyond a call of duty.

"Atwell is the bait for Sabine. I'm expecting that Sabine will have to verify the veracity of Atwell's claims. She will go after you, seeing you as an easy mark with your past history. If I'm not mistaken, she is very high in Fouche's network. As Napoleon's Minister of Police, Fouche exploits the situation of penniless aristocratic women with no family to work for him. I want the big fish. The one orchestrating the entire spy network in London. The contact in Dover is a small player. For Fouche, I surmise, Atwell was for short-term gains."

Jack quickened his pace, wearing a path in the deep rug. "There has to be another way. Abbie will be humiliated. I won't allow my wife to suffer public ridicule."

"You underestimate your wife. She is very capable of making the decision herself."

Red spots sparked before Jack's eyes—talk about being played. Rathbourne was the master of gamesmanship.

"You bloody—" Jack spun around. He didn't have much time before one of the soldier/footmen would intervene, but he was going to enjoy seeing the sight of blood spurting out of Rathbourne's haughty, aquiline nose. "All that sharing about our wives was an act to manipulate me."

Rathbourne slowly rose from his desk, and despite his sedentary ways, his well-defined muscles bunched across his waistcoat. He was still in prime shape, which made it all the better for Jack who wanted a bloody, sweaty fight, not an easy take-down. Fighting was much simpler in Jack's world than all this maneuvering and manipulating.

Rathbourne slowly came from behind the desk. "I meant every word I said. And if I'm not mistaken, you will be witness to my wife's strong will." He shrugged his shoulders, his voice even and calm. "She has taken it upon herself to protect Abbie from my scheme."

Jack still felt he had been duped. He clenched his fists at his sides, staring into Rathbourne's inscrutable eyes. He took one step closer, still wanting to wipe the smug smile off his face.

The door swung open. Henrietta marched in with Abbie following. "I told you that Jack was going to pummel my husband."

CHAPTER THREE

Abbie trailed Lady Henrietta through the long hallway lined with oil paintings of Lord Rathbourne's exalted descendants.

Henrietta, Jack's childhood friend, had come storming into the office, convinced that Jack was about to fight with Lord Rathbourne and that the women needed to intervene.

Even her hot-headed husband had enough sense to not attack the Head of England's Intelligence. Lord Rathbourne was guarded by very large and very intimidating soldiers.

Abbie reluctantly followed Lady Henrietta, disappointed by the lady's interruption of a very enlightening discussion with Lord Kendal about the 5th century B.C. Spartan's scytale—a transposition cipher.

Should Abbie be worried about her husband getting into a fight? Although Jack's hair was a deep mahogany, he, like the rest of the red-haired Bonnington males, held true to the myth that red-headed blood ran hotter. She quickened her pace at the memory of a Bonnington's instinctive reactions.

She should have recognized this morning, with her husband's absurd accusation about her and Lord Kendal, that her over-protective husband was worried. Jack had been shaken more deeply than she by her kidnapping. She'd never doubted Jack would rescue her, but it had frightened her husband and she was learning that Jack dealt with his fear by trying to exert his powerful will over the people he loved.

They had their first real fight after Jack had wanted to keep her secluded at his estate so no one could harm her. Jack revealed that his father's inability to function after his wife's death played into his overprotectiveness of Abbie. With the insight that Jack didn't doubt her capabilities but acted out of fear, Abbie had compromised with Jack's plans to guard her.

Her husband loved fiercely, unabashedly, and had no difficulty expressing his strong feelings. Growing up with cold, critical parents, Abbie had fallen in love with her husband's open affection and protectiveness toward his family. Unlike her father, who only saw his daughters as a means to fill his well-endowed coffers or elevate their family lineage.

Abbie froze in the doorway. It was clear from her husband's flushed face and clenched fists that he was rip-roaring mad. She had only seen Jack in a rage once, when he had confronted her kidnapper. Judging from the taut muscles under the confines of his gentleman's clothing, Jack was readying to fight. Although she had never witnessed Jack in a pub brawl, the younger Bonnington boys often regaled her with stories of Jack's combative escapades.

"Jack, what in heavens?"

Although the strained lines in Jack's face relaxed and his fists opened, he stayed in a fighting stance.

Lady Henrietta smoothly slipped in front of her husband. "I know why you want to punch him, Jack. He would do the same if the roles were reversed." She touched her husband's cheek. "Isn't that so, Cord?"

"Henrietta, this is Crown business." Lord Rathbourne

drew Lady Henrietta back against him. "And you should never place yourself between two men about to fight."

To Abbie's relief, Jack chuckled. "Hen has loads of experience stopping me and Kendal from pounding each other to a pulp."

Abbie realized she was still standing in the doorway, preventing the footman/soldier from closing the door. She took two steps into the room to avert the rest of the household from viewing the ensuing drama.

"Darling." Jack rushed to Abbie. "You don't have to do anything he says. We will find another way."

Jack wrapped his arm around her shoulder, holding her tight against him in a primitive, possessive way. "Rathbourne, I will not allow you to browbeat my wife. She need not sacrifice her happiness for the Crown's business."

"My God, Bonnington, you need to take up the stage. Talk about dramatic hyperbole."

Abbie felt Jack's body tense. Abbie's heart sped up, and her breath came in short spurts. Why was Lord Rathbourne provoking Jack? It was so out of character for her in-control, calm superior. And what could Lord Rathbourne ask her to do that would cause such an extreme reaction from Jack and Lady Henrietta?

Jack escorted Abbie to the one of the two chairs but remained standing next to her.

"Jack, can you please explain what is going on? I feel as if I've come into the second act of a Greek drama."

"My bloody point," Lord Rathbourne growled.

"Language, Cord. Abbie didn't grow up with the crude language of supposed gentlemen." Lady Henrietta turned toward Abbie. "Growing up with an older brother does help one appreciate the boorish methods males employ to settle their differences."

"Henrietta, do you want to sit next to Abbie?" Rathbourne offered his arm to his wife.

Lady Henrietta took his arm as she leaned against Lord Rathbourne's big frame. "No, I prefer standing next to you, my dear." She smiled up at her husband who raised one eyebrow. Some unspoken message was being shared between the couple.

Henrietta turned in her husband's arms to face Abbie. "There has been new information. Sabine Aubert is suspected of being the center of a French spy ring in London. My husband wants her to attend your Christmas house party to expose her by using Lord Atwell, her lover, as the bait."

Of all the possible requests, this hadn't come close to her imaginings when she decoded the newest message that Sabine, her husband's ex-mistress, was the possible spy. Abbie's first house party was to become a covert operation? How exciting and how much more interesting than planning the menu, the activities, and the decorations.

"Is that what all of this is about? Our house party?"

Lord Rathbourne started to speak but his wife elbowed him in the ribs.

Jack bent over Abbie. "Do you understand the scandal that will follow Sabine's appearance at *our* house?"

"Why would anyone care now since she isn't your mistress any longer?" Abbie twisted the fabric on her wool gown, trying hard to hide what discipline it took to speak unaffectedly.

Now that she was versed in the mystery of what occurred in the bedroom between men and women, Abbie didn't want to ever think about Jack with other women, especially Sabine, who was skilled in the art of seduction.

Abbie could feel Jack's eyes boring into her. Still, she couldn't look at him. He would know how hard this was to act sophisticated when she was madly in love with him and wouldn't want Sabine's presence as a reminder of his past. And how much it hurt her to imagine Jack sharing his fierce and passionate lovemaking with other women.

"Who will care? Are you joking?" Jack's voice pitched straight back into hostility. "All of society and my sister…well, probably not my sister." He paused. "But Aunt Mabel will never allow Sabine to attend. She is a stickler for protocol."

The aunt of Amelia's husband, Lord Brinsley, had been helpful in arranging Abbie's debut to society. She was one of the matrons who deemed who was accepted in good society and who was not. The bossy woman had shown her softer side to Abbie, probably because of the close friendship that had developed between Abbie and Amelia. Nonetheless, Sabine's attendance would be pushing the grand lady's sense of propriety.

"And what of your parents? Do you think your parents will countenance attending or allowing your sisters to attend?" Jack added.

Abbie must have moaned out loud since the room grew silent. She looked over at the Rathbournes. "My parents can be difficult."

Jack snorted with her understatement.

"Cord, I think Aunt Euphemia should be invited. She can—"

"I've already invited her."

"Of all the nerve, Rathbourne." Jack moved toward Lord Rathbourne. "This is Abbie's party. She decides who to invite."

"Jack, that is fine with me. I feel very close to Aunt Euphemia. She was the one who comforted me when you were injured."

Aunt Euphemia had been very insightful about Jack's nature, revealing how, at a young age, Jack had stepped into managing the estate and his younger siblings after his father's despair at the death of his adored wife had led him to withdraw from his family and estate business. His rakish past was part of his reaction to the loss of his mother, and, subsequently, his father.

"My Aunt Euphemia is an added safeguard for Abbie, in addition to all the usual protection."

"You must be joking," Jack seethed. "How is an old woman able to protect Abbie?"

Abbie looked up at Jack. "He means against society matrons. Isn't that correct, Lord Rathbourne?"

Lady Henrietta laughed. "Not at all. He means Aunt Euphemia will bodily protect you."

Abbie's mouth hung open. "Aunt Euphemia?"

"You're telling us that Aunt Euphemia is trained…trained in what?"

"My aunt is a very talented woman with many years of experience in covert operations, long before any of us were thus engaged. You shouldn't underestimate her. Mrs. Bonnington, am I to understand that you agree to my plans?" Lord Rathbourne queried.

"Before Abbie agrees, tell her how you are setting Sabine up to believe that I'm creating a new design to hide an explosive device in the tunnels of Dover in case we are invaded by the French. I will be telling Atwell that, and he will share that with his mistress. So, Sabine's aim at the party will be to search our house and to entice plans out of me."

Abbie kept her hands still and her gaze down, ignoring the clamoring turmoil. She didn't believe for a second Jack would betray her. He was too loyal, but might he be tempted? Many married men before him had mistresses, including her own father. Sabine was a beautiful woman, an acclaimed actress, and confident of her charm.

"Is Jack supposed to be receptive to Sabine's attention?"

"Bloody hell," Jack growled.

"Were you aware of the new message that Lord Kendal and I have been deciphering?" Abbie directed her attention to Lord Rathbourne and not her glowering husband.

"I was aware that we recovered a message."

Abbie never asked about the "how" of the recovery of messages. A shiver of apprehension snaked its way up her spine. Thankfully, she was spared the violent aspect of the business of espionage. "I have no definite proof, but the new message has very ornate penmanship which may have been written by a woman. The writer is asking for instructions on how to proceed. Is it a possibility that it was written by Sabine, asking for instructions on how to proceed in dealing with Lord Atwell?"

She tried not to stare at Lord Rathbourne's wide grin transforming the daunting superior into a dashing rogue. "That's it. Our strategy for the house party is perfect."

Lady Henrietta moved away from her husband's side to sit next to Abbie. The brilliant lady gently coddled Abbie's hand. "You don't have to go along with my husband's plan. He will figure out another means. Isn't that so, Cord? You appreciate all the work Abbie does already for our country."

"Naturally, I appreciate her work. And, there is always another method." Lord Rathbourne glared at his wife.

"This is the best way to trap Sabine?"

"This is the most expedient tactic and, most likely, the least deadly. We would allow Sabine to take the fictional weapon plans and then track her to her superior. Her superior is a key player in France's spy presence in London."

"May I have a minute with my husband, Lord Rathbourne? I'd like us to agree before I make a decision."

Henrietta tugged on her husband's arm. "Of course, Abbie. We will take this time to see baby Charles."

Lord Rathbourne stopped at the door. "Bonnington, shall I have my fencing master prepare a bout?"

Abbie didn't like the gleam in Jack's smile. "By all means, I'll look forward to crossing swords."

CHAPTER FOUR

Abbie tucked her dress before standing. This wasn't a mutual exchange with her forceful husband towering over her. Jack pulled her up against him, wrapping his chiseled arms around her. "Abbie, I'm sorry I was an ass. I acted like a complete idiot this morning. I thought Rathbourne was going to send me to Dover, leaving you unprotected, and I was…" His voice was gritty with emotion.

That was not the response Abbie had expected. She thought Jack would badger her into refusing to help trap Sabine. He had such old-fashioned concepts about women. She was a code breaker working for England's spy network. She was going to do her job, no matter who the spy might be. Indeed, as Abbie adjusted to the prospect of Sabine at her house party, she was envisioning the pleasure in besting the woman at her own game.

Jack took her mouth with a searing kiss. He whispered against her lips, "It seems I'm going to be apologizing a great deal in our marriage. I act like a crazy man when it comes to you."

"Why didn't you tell me about the possibility of a Dover assignment?" Abbie demanded, refusing to be distracted by the sensual promise in Jack's eyes.

He brushed one of her curls behind her ear, his gentle touch lingering. "Because I didn't want you to worry."

Abbie gave an exasperated laugh. "Instead, you concluded that working closely with Lord Kendal would inevitably lead to us having an affair."

"Abbie, I don't want you near Sabine. She's a treacherous French spy. Capable of anything. I was completely fooled."

"Yes, you were." She couldn't mask the bitterness in her voice. "Not any different than any than other man." Abbie backed away from Jack, away from the gnawing sting of jealousy. How strange to feel betrayed when she wasn't acquainted with Jack when he was involved with Sabine?

She clung to her belief that her husband was starting to view women as different from his *gentleman's* preconceived and antiquated notions of women and their role in society.

"Abbie." He caught her bare hand, pressed it hard to his mouth, greedily savoring her sensitive skin. "Sabine means nothing to me. She never did."

Abbie drew away with a small painful laugh and turned toward the ceiling-high rows of books. Her heart pounded as she pretended to examine the titles. She could trust Jack, couldn't she? The ugly darkness of doubt was seeping down deep into her fear of men and the power they wielded over women. Jack wasn't like her father. She tried to reassure herself but couldn't quell her anxiety.

Despite the temptation of her husband's seductive, loving eyes, she couldn't shake the need to protect herself, learned too well in childhood from dealing with her father's mercurial nature and tyrannical authority. Running a finger along the spine of one of the leather-bound tomes, she asked, "Did you know Lord Rathbourne moved the library from Lady Henrietta's family estate to Rathbourne house as a wedding present for her?"

"That doesn't sound like the cold, calculating bastard."

Abbie spun quickly to face her husband. "What did Lord Rathbourne mean by meeting him later? You aren't going to duel with him?"

"No. We're just going to brandish our swords." Jack waggled his eyebrows, waiting for Abbie to catch on to his innuendo. He had taught her all the slang words men used for their body. Abbie's education about men and their desires was on a fast, upward curve, but not nearly fast enough to catch up with her husband's vast experience. Although Jack was pushing her to use "naughty" words during their lovemaking, she wasn't close to saying the words aloud.

Abbie flashed on how Sabine probably wouldn't struggle with saying anything in bed and turned back to the books. The title at eye-level was "Mabinogion, Ancient Welsh Romances." She suppressed a harsh laugh. Instead of reading Euclid, she should have been reading more about romance. She lacked both experience and knowledge to make sense of her feelings, a Gordian knot of love and devotion, insecurity and hostility.

"We're not going to duel, merely working out our manly frustrations. From what Kendal says, Rathbourne had a more notorious reputation than mine or Brinsley's for excesses and brawling."

"Is that what you call Sabine? An excess?" Abbie continued to stare at the books but saw only Jack and Sabine entangled in bed, enjoying excess. She shut her eyes tight, like a child believing that if you closed your eyes, a terrifying vision would disappear.

"Abbie." Jack pulled her back against him again, her body fitting perfectly against his hard strength. His stubble rubbed along her neck, creating a frisson of awareness. "I wish I could go back in time and change my past. I wish I had not acquired the reputation of a rake…even if mild in comparison to my peers. None of that matters. Nothing matters except that I love you."

"You expect me to believe that you never cared about Sabine." Abbie spoke to the books. "She is beautiful and a renowned actress."

Jack drew her to him. "Abbie, you are the only woman I have loved. And the only one I ever will."

Abbie wanted to believe Jack. "I'm sure all men say that to their wives." She had always wondered if her strong-willed mother had ever confronted her husband about his mistress.

"Damn it, Abbie." His voice softened. "You're too innocent to understand about men and mistresses."

"But…" Abbie couldn't bring herself to ask if Jack compared their lovemaking to his other women. It would hurt too much to hear an honest response. Her confident, rakish husband would never understand her insecurity about his past with beautiful women. Abbie was a scholar, not a stunning beauty. Her mother had told her matter-of-factly that her looks were not of the first order. By Amelia's account, her brother had had been involved with a wide swathe of stunning women across London. She reminded herself that she had other talents that Jack valued.

"You're right." Abbie heard the brittleness in her voice. "It doesn't matter. It's all in the past." Abbie didn't want to discuss Jack's mistresses or her lack of worldly experience since no words would reassure her. What she had to do was concentrate on the purpose of Sabine's presence at the party. Besides, she did believe "in theory" that women shouldn't denigrate the choices made by other women. Until now, she never had a need to put into practice that lofty ideal. She had no illusions that Sabine's attendance at the party would be challenging. Still, this was war. And it was most likely Sabine was key to unraveling the spy ring. Abbie would do her best to stop the French.

Jack twirled her curls between his fingers. "You don't understand because you're a loving, caring woman. Sabine is a manipulative witch. She's incapable of caring for anyone but herself."

"So, why did you choose a creature like that? You're as bad as she is."

Jack flinched at Abbie's harsh tone. "Because I didn't want…I didn't want to lose myself like my father. Sabine is not the kind of woman I would ever care about."

Abbie ran her fingers along Jack's sculpted cheekbones. "Your mother's death took a terrible toll on your entire family." She understood that Jack had been shaped by his father's failings, just as she had been by her own father's.

"My mother was a lively woman who kept us all together. After her death, I vowed to never let a woman have a hold on me. I became involved with Sabine to keep up my rakish reputation. Nothing more. She was the one woman every man wanted. It is a game that idle gentlemen play. There was no genuine feeling between us."

Abbie couldn't grasp the world that Jack had lived in. As a woman, she didn't have a choice, bending to society's expectation that she make a good match to assure her future. For women, it was survival; for men, a game—one that Jack had excelled at.

Even though she fervently believed Mary Wollstonecraft's assertion that women were not inferior to men but kept so by their lack of education, Abbie hadn't rebelled against her parents' demands. Instead, she was fortunate to fall in love and be married to a man she loved and who valued her mind and independent spirit. Nonetheless, it wasn't easy to face Jack's rakish past. "What different lives we've led. It is difficult," Abbie said with a sigh.

"Not difficult now. What matters now is our life together. You came storming into my life, disagreeing with everything I said, making me look at my jaded world and how little it meant to me." Jack gave his playful wolfish grin that always melted her. "I couldn't resist you. What a lonely shallow life I led until I met you."

Abbie didn't want to dwell on the past. She couldn't imagine life without Jack. She loved her husband. "I'm glad you waited for me, Jack Bonnington." Rakish past or not, he was a loyal son, brother, and husband, and she knew in her heart he would not betray her.

Rather than comparing herself to Sabine, Abbie had to keep her focus on the important work she and Jack were doing. She was proud that her husband was changing his perceptions of women because of her success at code-breaking. And handling this mission with Sabine would be more proof of her capabilities. "Jack, we must do what Lord Rathbourne asks and have Sabine as a houseguest."

"Are you sure, my darling?"

"We have to intervene if we can."

Jack kissed the top of her head, holding her against him. "I assumed you would agree."

"Why, then, were you arguing with Lord Rathbourne, ready to fight with him?"

"Because I wanted to make it clear that you had a choice. And that Rathbourne and I aren't done discussing his manipulations."

Abbie wrapped her arms around his waist. "Promise me you won't hurt him."

Jack gave a rueful laugh. "Thank you for your faith in me, dear wife."

Abbie savored the closeness of this moment. The house party certainly was going to be complicated to manage. "I don't know who is going to be more difficult for me to handle: Sabine or my mother."

"We will face them together."

Jack's words and caresses comforted her. It strengthened her resolve, knowing he was there to share her burdens. "I believe it best not to call attention to Sabine's attendance but to be as cordial to her as to all our guests."

"Cordial? I'd like to wring her bloody neck for putting us into this situation. And for using me to get to Kendal."

"Exactly why we need to be cordial. It is the only way not to raise her suspicions."

"Abbie Lyon Bonnington, you are a scary woman." Jack teased the seam of her lips with his tongue. "I hope you'll never plot against me."

"Then you had better be just playing a "part" with Sabine," Abbie teased.

CHAPTER FIVE

Sabine couldn't bear the sight of Atwell's blotchy red face as he thrust over and over into her one second longer so she squeezed her eyes shut. Gasping for air and grunting with the exertion, he may well have been in his death throes. The obese earl couldn't die before she got what she was after.

Her closed eyes didn't diminish his foul, hot breath blowing in her face, his sweaty chest slipping and rubbing against her, and his ridiculous barely hard cock. It was almost too much to endure, even though he inevitably came to a quick finish.

Still, she had endured more than one stupid man. She was alive because she had endured. Atwell was into pain and enjoyed her whippings, however, it took away any pleasure she might enjoy inflicting it, knowing it gave him gratification when she wanted men like him to suffer as she had.

Playing games with rich, overbred English aristocrats was nothing compared to torture by Fouche's men. All went smoothly in her life until Fouche's men discovered her leaving France with forged papers. They tortured her to learn about her noble employers and where they might keep their wealth until she confessed to something grave. Serving as the vicomtesse's maid for years had made it easy to kill the bitch. When Fouche, France's Minister of Police, had learned of her audacity in killing the Vicomtesse of Perigueux then taking her papers to escape France, he recruited her for his web of spies.

Now, she served the brutal Minister of Police bringing down the English aristocrats. She had learned many secrets from English gentlemen in their cups or in the throes of sexual encounter—gentlemen who didn't expect a mere woman, a whore at that, capable of understanding, let alone using, the information.

With one final grunt, Atwell collapsed on top of her, his weight crushing her. She gripped the bedsheets to restrain herself from snapping Atwell's neck and ending this charade. She had acquired many skills under the tutelage of her mentor, Luc Duval. "Atwell, my dear, have you fallen asleep?" She shoved hard against the barely conscious walrus. The imbecile had drunk too much. "You said you had something important to tell me."

She needed information about Dover Castle fortifications for Napoleon was in the midst of preparing plans for the French invasion of England. For the last while, the information passed on by Atwell has been suspiciously unreliable. Equally suspicious was the death of his partner in embezzlement, Lieutenant Hyde, who had also been stealing secrets about the Dover fortification plans and routing them to the French. Atwell being designated as his replacement by the Committee was just too much of a coincidence. Atwell didn't know that Sabine knew he was the one now selling secrets to the French. He considered himself quite masterful at the spy game, not realizing his usefulness for either side would be of very short duration.

She shoved again and he finally rolled off of her.

He exhaled loudly, his voice still breathless. "Sabine, tell me who is the better cocksman? Me or Bonnington?"

Sabine covered her mouth, attempting to stifle her urge to laugh. Bonnington had been a generous and considerate lover, unlike any of the others. It had been hard to leave him for Atwell who required punishment for gratification.

"Darling, there is no comparison." And then Sabine almost did laugh. It was probably the first time in a long time she had said anything truthful.

"I've come up with a plan for us to be together." He rolled to one side, his bloated stomach keeping their bodies from touching.

"We are together." Men were ridiculous and such infants.

"My plan is to escape to France where you will be treated equally, not like here where gentlemen would never introduce you to their wives."

For running a very successful embezzling scheme, the man never saw beyond his privileged life. As if she wanted to mingle with Atwell's wife and the other haughty women in society.

Why would she return to France? Under Luc's tutelage, she managed the entire network of spies operating in London and she enjoyed the irony of being considered an "untouchable" by the English women when their husbands did more than touch her while they gave away their country's secrets.

"You're an English peer. How could you possibly want to leave England and give up your title?"

"I met Bonnington at the club the other night. Usually, he can hold his liquor but his marriage had him in his cups. Like all men of title, he did his duty, but I guess the dew is off the flower. Except, I must say," Atwell chuckled, "I'd taste the honey of his little wife anytime."

So Bonnington, a demanding and daring lover, was already tired of his English rose of a wife. That was excellent news that she would put to good use.

Sabine yanked Atwell's nipple hard. "Are you being a bad boy, talking about another woman?" Atwell's lips twisted into a pleased grimace.

"I need you, Sabine. I've made a mess of my life and I want to escape. Run away with me."

What was Atwell up to?

"What does Bonnington have to do with us leaving England?"

"Bonnington let it slip that he has been working on a new explosive that will be hidden in Dover's tunnels. He said it is his idea alone, and he's going to present it to the Dover Battlement Committee after the holidays. I could steal the plans at his party and use them to barter with the French for our escape. I have some connections with several highly-placed Frenchmen whom I'm sure would pay a handsome sum for such plans."

For the first time that night, Sabine smiled genuinely.

"You'll live in luxury. I have enough money hidden away for us to live in style in France."

She lived in luxury in London. And it was intriguing that Atwell was asserting that he had money hidden away since her contacts maintained that the man was in debt.

Was this a set-up to trap Atwell or her? Atwell was too self-centered to see beyond his own needs. And although a gratifying lover, Bonnington didn't have any connection to English Intelligence to make her believe he was orchestrating this new scheme. She had tried to gather information from him but Bonnington was exactly as he appeared—a bored, titled gentleman who had no concept that England was at war or that his way of life was about to end.

"What a clever man you are." Sabine yanked both his nipples. "I might have to use the clamps later for being so clever."

"Sabine, say you'll escape with me."

"I think I'll go to the party and help you."

"I don't think I can bring you." God, men were tiresome. Idiots. "My wife. And Bonnington won't tolerate it."

"Bonnington and I are dear friends. I think I'll have Cosgrove invite me." She was sure she could find a way to convince Captain Cosgrove, who had been waiting for her most every night after her performances, to finagle an invitation since he was friends with Bonnington.

"We have to be careful. Bonnington isn't a fool."

"I'm sure you'll come up with a foolproof plan," Sabine cooed.

CHAPTER SIX

Hearing the sound of his new bride's laughter echoing in the hallways made concentrating on the estate's finances, a tedious task under any circumstances, impossible, so Jack left his office in search of Abbie, leaving his father to finish the review. It was only three days until the Christmas Eve ball, and Jack wanted to spend as much time with his wife before the fateful evening.

Climbing the stairs, he found Abbie giggling, with her younger sister Eliza by her side in the ballroom. Together, with the aid Aunt Mabel and her stuffy butler Hotchkiss, they were transforming Bonnington estate into a festive holiday palace. Abbie was breathing new life into his home, and he wanted to share in her excitement and pleasure for the Christmas season as only a husband could.

His idea was to steal his wife away to their secret hut before all the holiday guests descended upon them tomorrow for the house party. The recently installed cast-iron stove in the forester's hut had been lit. And hopefully was burning brightly.

It was time to prove to his wife he loved her and would never stray. He hadn't missed Abbie's struggle when they had discussed Sabine's attendance. Abbie didn't trust men. Jack couldn't blame her after meeting her father. The man saw women as having one purpose—to serve his needs: his wife to provide heirs, his daughters to increase his coffers, and his mistresses to please him. No wonder Abbie was struggling to trust Jack. And it didn't help that Jack's past was checkered. Even after his revelation to Abbie that these casual affairs were his way of keeping true intimacy and the pain of caring too deeply at bay, he acknowledged that Abbie still questioned whether Jack's past was proof that he resembled her father.

Jack leaned on the doorjamb, enjoying the sight of his wife, her dress clinging to all the curves he appreciated, her white-blond curls hanging over her eyes escaping from her top knot as she bent over spools of ribbon. Eliza's resemblance to Abbie was remarkable; they had the same blond curls, bright blue eyes, and trim figures. The main difference was that Eliza had no interest in the scholarly pursuits pursued with zeal by her older sister. Eliza's interests lay in horses and horse-riding.

Amelia and Hotchkiss were on the far side of the ballroom.

"Abbie, come give your opinion on where the orchestra stage should be," Amelia called out. "Hotchkiss and I agree that it should be away from the French doors and far enough away from the entrance to not block the flow of guests. What do you think?"

"Amelia, you know I have no opinion." Abbie laughed.

Jack couldn't resist teasing his wife. "This doesn't sound like my wife. Eliza, Amelia, Hotchkiss, what have you done with Mrs. Bonnington?"

Abbie's look of joyous surprise made Jack all the more pleased for his foresight in arranging today's diversion. "Jack! I thought you were doing finances with your father."

"I was. Now that my father is managing part of the estate, it doesn't take as long to review with him. I'm here on a mission that requires your assistance." Jack knew he'd seize Abbie's attention by throwing out the word "mission."

"Right now?" Abbie searched his face, looking for clues whether it might be a command from Rathbourne.

"Meet me at the front door. Bundle up for out of doors."

Abbie bustled across the room, her errant curls bouncing on her shoulders, making it hard for Jack to breathe when he pictured how her curls brushed across his chest in the throes of their lovemaking. He tried to keep his expression neutral. His wife was becoming adept at reading his boundless lust.

"Jack, I can't leave now." Breathless from rushing, her voice got husky, as when she had begged him…this morning. Heat flooded through his body. He was in bad shape if he couldn't wait hours until he had Abbie again. Would he ever not desire his wife desperately?

Abbie eyed him. He must have given her some clue of his carnal intentions. "We're in the middle of decorating."

"Go with Jack. Hotchkiss and I can handle everything, especially with Eliza's help. "Put my brother out of his misery." Amelia waved her off.

It was a good thing Jack had prepped Amelia ahead of time on his plans.

"Usually, I enjoy my brother's misery." Amelia shook her fiery mane. "It must be the holiday spirit." She winked at him.

"This is important, Abbie. Meet me at the front door in five minutes." And, with that, Jack walked out the door before his wife could badger him into revealing his surprise.

Donning his greatcoat, Jack waited at the bottom of the stairs with Abbie's Christmas present tucked under his arm.

He heard her hurried steps along the upstairs floor and

then watched as she descended the stairs, first staring at his face and then at the large wrapped box trailing red ribbons. Amelia had wrapped the present with her usual flair. And how it had annoyed his sister to not know what was inside the box. He wanted Abbie to be the first to see her present. And what were irritating younger sisters for, if not to torment?

Jack stepped forward and offered his other arm to Abbie.

"Who is the present for? Is it a peace offering for Lord Rathbourne?"

Jack laughed. How Abbie could presume he'd buy Rathbourne a present was beyond him. Just because Jack had won their fencing duel didn't mean he felt bad. No, Jack had taken great pleasure in besting his superior. Rathbourne, however, had just seen it as further proof that Jack had all the requisite skills for a great agent.

Jack would never admit, even on pain of death, that if Rathbourne had been ten years younger, he might not have bested him. The man handled himself very well for being in his forties.

Jack assisted Abbie down the outside stairs. The day was clear and cold, unusual for an English December, which usually meant gray skies and rain.

"You're acting very mysterious." Abbie peered up at him through her thick eyelashes. "And are you going to tell me who the present is for?"

Jack knew he was straightforward and brutally honest to a fault, but he'd like to feel he was capable of a few surprises. His wife was making him sound boring, predictable, and stodgy. Wait until he stripped his wife of her clothes.

"Is there new information about Lord Atwell and Sabine? Is that why Lord Rathbourne has summoned us?"

Jack was willing to share his first surprise. "Yes, Rathbourne and I came to an agreement." Jack liked how reasonable that sounded. She would strongly disapprove if she knew the agreement was if Jack won the fencing joust, Rathbourne would arrange for Sabine to attend only the Christmas Eve ball and not the house party. The prospect of Sabine sleeping in his house, near his wife, fired his blood to decimate Rathbourne in their fencing match.

"Sabine will not be attending our house party."

Abbie stopped and put her hands on her hips. "I thought we agreed it was imperative for her to tend."

"It was imperative we give her a chance to steal the plans. And she will have time and opportunity to steal them at the ball. The fake plans that I've drawn up will be in my locked desk. It will not be a difficult task for Sabine to pick the lock. Cosgrove, Sabine's escort for the ball, and his underlying will watch Sabine and Atwell and apprehend them once they've stolen them. Rathbourne and his minions are handling all the details. All we need to do is host the party." Jack didn't add, "and dodge Sabine."

"Why am I getting a strange feeling that this change has something to do with you beating Lord Rathbourne?"

As usual, his wife was quick to make the right deduction. Other men might feel threatened, but not Jack. He was proud of his wife's prodigious talents.

Abbie had continued to work early in the morning, deciphering the increasing volume of messages from Napoleon's pressing invasion. She didn't need to make social chit-chat with an evil woman with malevolent intentions. His wife was pure goodness and didn't need to face evil in her own house, especially at this time of year of peace and goodwill.

"Darling, let's leave it as a gentlemen's agreement, shall we?"

Abbie sighed loudly and squeezed Jack's arm. "It is great news. Thank you, Jack. I don't want to know what you did to

Lord Rathbourne. Either way, I'm very grateful to have a husband who cares so dearly about my welfare."

A loving Abbie was beaming at him as if he had fought Napoleon singlehandedly and won the war.

"And there are more surprises." Jack steered Abbie off the main path to the renovated hut. Smoke billowed out of the new brick chimney. Jack had seen to the all the details, including the mammoth bed that graced the tiny space. There was to be no more discomfort when he made love to his wife.

"Jack, I thought we had to meet with Lord Rathbourne?"

"No, that was a little ruse to steal my wife away before the guests arrive."

"The hut has a new chimney and a new roof?"

"All part of my Christmas presents for my wife." Jack opened the door to the heated hut.

Abbie's eyes widened in astonishment at the Persian rugs across the wood floor and the bed covered in the finest linens.

Jack took her into his arms. "Do you approve of my surprise?"

"When did you have time to do all this? And how did you keep it a secret from me?" The awe in Abbie's voice captivated Jack.

"Abbie, I will never forget your seduction in this hut. It was the best gift any man could ever receive. And I will do my best to always honor the generosity of your gift of love that you gave me that day. Expect to be showered with presents, my darling wife."

Jack was eager to give Abbie the best gift that would make them both joyful for the season. "Your next present requires you to take off your clothes."

Abbie giggled. "Jack Bonnington. Is that what you're calling it now?"

Abbie hadn't a clue how she inflamed his desire just by

the way her lips curled into laughter or the little noise of appreciation she made in her throat before she lost herself in orgasm.

"Let me help you." He slipped his wife's pelisse off and threw it over a chair. He turned her to release the ties on the back of her gown. The subtle scent of her hair, the touch of her skin beneath his hands heightened his burning need. Making fast work of the rest of her clothes, he lifted her into his arms.

The touch of her soft skin, the scent of Abbie, was all he needed in this world. He couldn't stop his hands from searching for his favorite crevices.

Abbie wrapped her arms around his neck while rubbing her soft breasts against him. From how she was lightly panting, it was clear she was enjoying the rough friction from his waistcoat.

"This isn't fair. Why am I to be the only one naked?"

"So impatient?" He lowered her to the bed, reveling in the glorious sight of Abbie naked.

She scrambled on her knees to the head of the bed. Did his innocent wife realize the view she had given him? The minx knew exactly what she was doing, pushing him to the brink.... His plans for his wife's slow seduction hadn't considered his wife's fervid response.

She fluffed the pillows and then positioned herself with her hands clasped over one knee, upping the game between them.

Her rapt attention on his groin, tenting in his breeches, pushed him to the edge. He kicked off his boots and ripped off his breeches and drawers in one motion.

Her lips parted and her eyes flared wide, focusing on his erection, causing his member to throb and grow when her lips parted in appreciation.

"You're magnificent." Her chest rose and fell in soft, rapid anticipation.

She drew him to her with a power that enthralled him. His intention had been to demonstrate to Abbie that every moment with her was fresh and new. After his careful and full attention to her needs, she would never doubt his devotion.

He took her mouth with a voracious kiss, thrusting his tongue deep into her mouth. Abbie met him with her tongue sliding over his.

"Abbie, we're off our schedule."

"We have a schedule?" Abbie threw one leg over his hip and he was lost. His stubborn wife had her own plans, and Jack was finding it very easy to comply.

She ground against him, her heat surrounding him. His heart thumped against his chest as all the blood flowed south. "I'm ravenous to taste you and determined to make this last as long as I can."

Her sudden shiver helped Jack remember his agenda. He bent to her breasts, molding the luscious mounds in his hands, loving the whimpers she made as he licked the raspberry-colored nipples, and how her legs moved restlessly against his as he drew one nipple in and sucked on it with a wet swirl of his tongue.

"Jack," she moaned, arching her back, offering him more.

He switched to her other breast, this time less gently. Abbie gasped his name again as she rocked her hips against him. Jack grew harder, aching for her hot, wet welcome.

He moved down her body, inspired by Abbie's whimper of protest, sucking on her porcelain white skin, marking her with love bites that only he would see.

He came up to his knees between her legs and leaned to give her the barest brush of his lips against her pale thigh. He spread her legs wider, giving him his favorite invitation. Her pink sex, hidden in blond curls, was slick with excitement. "The only thing I could focus on during the estate review was getting you to this hut, to this moment again. You, screaming my name."

Jack sunk his fingers into her soft thighs and used his thumb to part her lips. She was wet, glistening. He bent over and licked her center, inhaling her arousal. He flicked her nub with the tip of his tongue, teasing her while watching color engulf her face and her breathing change to pants.

"Jack, please," she pleaded.

With the pads of his fingertips, he stroked, sliding and tantalizing.

"More, Jack."

He wanted to make this perfect for her. He lingered at her nub, laving her with his whole tongue. Abbie grabbed his hair and pushed her center deeper against his tongue. Her moans became more frantic as she arched her back. He pressed his tongue into her, pushing her over the edge. Her thighs trembled. She sobbed his name as the waves took her. He stayed with her, licking, gently bringing her down.

Abbie, with her eyes closed, her body lax and open against the pillows, her magnificent brain not spinning—this was his Christmas present for his wife. One he resolved to give her daily, with or without a holiday. He wanted to watch his wife lose control for the rest of their lives.

"Jack." Abbie opened her eyes and extended her arms for him.

He took his time, nipping his way back up her dewy body. He was committed to savoring the moment, wanting their afternoon interlude to go on forever.

"I need you inside me, Jack, please." Her blue eyes appeared brighter against the blush-stain of arousal coloring her cheeks.

Jack nuzzled her neck, licking along her throat, then he kissed her, drawing his tongue along her parted lips and opening her mouth to mate.

She clung to his neck, brushing her erect nipples back and forth against his chest, wrapping her legs around his waist, pushing her wet core against him in open invitation. His hips spasmed against her; his body poised to take her on a fast and furious ending. This wasn't what he wanted for her today.

Instead, he pulled her tight against him and rolled her on top of him. She now was draped over his chest, her thighs straddling him. He stared into her eyes. "Abbie, I love you and will always love you."

"I love you too. And you know what else I love is to have you inside me."

He laughed loudly. "Is that right? I haven't finished giving you my Christmas presents." Jack circled her nipples with his fingertips, watching her breath catch, her tongue darting in out of her mouth, her blond curls dancing across her chest.

Abbie moved against him, trying to entice him. "It isn't Christmas yet." Her words came out breathless.

She was already close, making his heart swell with love. He tugged on her nipple as he delved two fingers deep into her heat. Her body shuddered when he rotated his fingers. She threw her head back as she rode his fingers, crying out his name in her release. She collapsed on his chest.

Abbie's trust and total abandonment set Jack's body on fire. His body was hard and a trigger away from exploding. He couldn't wait any longer.

"How about I give you another Christmas present?" he murmured into her ear before flipping their positions so fast that she squeaked.

"No more Jack."

He covered her, reveling in the lush sensations of her slick hot body against his. The scent of her arousal curled through him. His erection throbbed next to her opening.

He kissed her gently. "Abbie, open your eyes." He took her mouth again, drunk with need as he slowly filled her.

"Watch us together, Abbie. This is me loving you. This is me needing you." He withdrew and pressed into her again. "Always needing you." Jack couldn't take his eyes off his wife's glowing face, overwhelmed by the acceptance and answering love in Abbie's eyes.

"I love you, Jack."

Abbie tightened her core, her snug sheath clasping him and taking him deeper into her body, pushing him out of control. His slow and shallow thrusts turned to fast and deep. He lowered his weight on his arms to change the angle, trying to wait for Abbie. With the change, Abbie moaned and dug her nails into his back.

Lost in the sensation of Abbie surrounding him, milking him, Jack thrust harder. Abbie met him, matching his rhythm until her body bowed and she screamed, taking Jack with her into their shattering release.

Jack collapsed on top of his wife, sated, barely able to breathe or think.

"Merry Christmas, Jack."

Jack raised his head to see Abbie's laughing eyes. "My Christmas present for you seems to have been well-received."

"If it were any better received, I'd be dead." Jack loved Abbie's smug and confident smile.

"I love you, Abbie Lyon Bonnington."

Abbie wiggled under Jack, seeming to have regained her strength before Jack. He was content to stay wrapped in the afterglow.

"Do I now get to open my present?"

Jack rolled off of his wife, knowing his weight was too much. This was the perfect time to drape his present over his wife's beautiful body. He stood to fetch the box.

Abbie propped the pillows behind her. "Amelia has been going on about your present for me. And how secretive you've been."

"You knew all along that the present was for you?"

"I wasn't sure since you implied that we had a meeting with Lord Rathbourne."

Jack sat with one hip on the side of the bed and handed Abbie her Christmas present.

Abbie's face blushed as she took the gift between her hands. "Thank you, Jack." She tugged at the ribbons to open the box. Her eyes widened as she reverently touched the ermine scarf and muff.

"They're beautiful." Abbie wrapped the scarf around her neck. "And perfect for the house party with the outdoor entertainments." She placed her hands into the muff. "How did you know?"

"Because you're my wife, and I'll always try to know what you need. Merry Christmas, Abbie."

"Merry Christmas, Jack." Abbie's lips curved into a small smile. "Are you ready for my present again?"

Laughing Jack climbed onto the bed and wrestled his wife down on the covers, nudging her with his erection. "I'm always ready for you."

CHAPTER SEVEN

Abbie and Jack, in their role as hosts of the ball, promenaded among their convivial holiday guests, the scent of pine from the hanging bows on the chandeliers, the flickering of the candles, and the sudden snowfall outside the large windows making the ballroom appear as magical as a scene in an enchanted fairy tale. For a moment, Abbie almost forgot that it was also a ruse to bait treasonous spies.

Abbie had rehearsed many times how she would graciously welcome Sabine, as she would all her other guests. Her effort was wasted. Arriving late with Captain Cosgrove, as Jack and Abbie greeted them in the guest line, Sabine merely nodded, barely acknowledging Abbie except for a snide remark about Abbie's dress.

Suddenly, Jack bent close and whispered in her ear. "Cosgrove is signaling me. I'll be right back. Don't go anywhere I can't see you."

She searched the room for her two bodyguards, Aunt Euphemia and Ford. Her short height was a disadvantage since she couldn't see over the crowd.

Almost nauseated from the anxiety of whether Sabine and Atwell had taken the bait, Abbie ignored her clamoring heart as she continued to stop and chat with the guests, trying not to watch the interaction between Jack and Captain Cosgrove at the door.

When Cosgrove departed, Abbie turned to make her way back to her husband, impatient to hear what Cosgrove had reported.

Jack gave her a subtle nod. And her stomach was off and spinning again. This game of cat and mouse wasn't her forte, especially when Sabine was the cat, playing with her husband. Although Abbie's sole role in tonight's scenario was to be the hostess, still she was having trouble suppressing her churning feelings.

"Abbie, take a deep breath," Jack murmured, his warm hand on her back, steadying her. "It's all under control. Sabine, in her pelisse and boots, is outside the Conservatory waiting for Atwell. Cosgrove is going to follow them."

Abbie knew Jack wasn't as calm as he tried to appear. His tension transmitted into Abbie as they glided into the crowd. The tension flowed between them, ripe with uncertainty. It took all her self-discipline to keep smiling and maintain social banter as she and Jack moved through the crowds.

"Your sister seems to be enjoying tonight's ball." Jack smoothed his hand on her arm to soothe and distract her.

Abbie followed Jack's glance. Aunt Mabel stood guard with her sister, Eliza, whose face beamed with excitement at attending her first ball. The ivory dress that Amelia designed for Eliza was perfect, showcasing her beautiful, nubile body. At Eliza's arrival, Abbie had been proud and amused to see all the gentlemen taking notice, even Captain Cosgrove who was definitely too old for her.

"I'm glad that my parents decided to stay in the country because of the inclement weather. I don't know if I could have handled the added pressure of my mother."

"You don't give yourself enough credit. Look around. Your first ball is a major success."

"That's very kind, Jack, but we both know it was Amelia, Aunt Mabel, and Hotchkiss who deserve the credit." Aunt Mabel had brought her well-organized butler to work with Mrs. Wells, the Bonningtons' housekeeper.

Jack steered her toward the chairs lining the walls for the elderly guests to enjoy the ball. While they waited for the news that Sabine and Atwell had been taken into custody, Jack stuck by her side to assure her that she wouldn't be at any risk. Abbie wasn't worried about her own safety; Jack would do everything to protect her. She was frightened for Jack and everyone she cared for.

Struggling to maintain her composure, she took a deep breath and inhaled the sweet pine smell of Christmas. Amelia, wanting the smell of the holiday to fill the space, had outdone herself with the abundant placement of pine boughs throughout the ballroom.

Abbie smiled at Lady Billingsworth, an entire ostrich of plumes positioned in her upswept hairstyle, with heavy strands of emeralds on her generous bosom. The two chairs next to her were unoccupied, as if she were holding court. The haughty matron harrumphed at Jack before turning her gaze at Abbie.

"Your mother would be very proud of your choice in your wife, young man. She is a true lady. It is admirable how she has handled the potential scandal from your scurrilous past."

Abbie's face flushed at the lady's remarks as she did a small curtsy. "Thank you, Lady Billingsworth, for joining us tonight to celebrate the holidays. I know you're a dear friend of Lady Stamford." Abbie had been instructed to mention Aunt Mabel with anyone who brought up Sabine's attendance.

"Did Mabel tell you that we came out together?" The woman sat ramrod straight, her back not touching the chair, her weight forward on a cane. "Poor Mabel, she was a little thing, but now…" Lady Billingsworth let the idea of Aunt Mabel's generous size take hold.

Jack squeezed Abbie's arm, which helped her to quell the giggle about to erupt. Lady Billingsworth was no fragile figure of a woman. Talk about the pot calling the kettle black. She was at least twelve stones.

Jack bent and kissed the grand lady's hand while gracing her with his dashing grin. "You're absolutely right, Lady Billingsworth. At this season, it is the time to reflect on the gifts we have in our lives, like your years of friendship with Lady Stamford. My lovely and understanding wife is better than any Christmas present I could wish for." Jack looked down at Abbie, his gaze filled with love. His possessive look turned her knees to jelly while heat rushed through her like a brush fire. Her husband safe from danger was the only Christmas present she wanted.

Lady Billingsworth tut-tutted at Jack and pointed her cane at Abbie. "Your gown is very unusual. The colors are 'different.'"

Having been raised by a highly critical mother, Abbie recognized the barb for what it was; a reflection of a lonely and unhappy woman. The poor lady's husband and only son had died.

"My sister is the designer, and she has done the unthinkable." Jack covered his lips and bent closer to Lady Billingsworth as if sharing a secret.

Amelia, a designer extraordinaire, had matched the burgundy ribbons intertwined with the ballroom's pine boughs to the appliques on Abbie's sky-blue dress. Amelia was adamant that Abbie wear blue to complement her eyes and had added the burgundy ribbons for the seasonal touch. The color and design came together perfectly. The dress was stunning, and Jack's appreciative stare when Abbie had descended the stairs was worth all of Amelia's demands.

Lady Billingsworth leaned forward on her cane, almost panting, like her little dogs, for the tidbit of gossip.

Abbie watched in admiration at Jack's ability to distract the gossipmonger. "She has accomplished something I didn't think possible. She has made my beautiful wife shine more beautifully than I thought possible. Mrs. Bonnington looks like a Christmas angel to be placed on the top of the Christmas tree."

Lady Billingsworth sat back in her chair and mumbled just loudly enough for them to hear about Jack always having a silver tongue.

Jack led Abbie away and turned her to him.

"Jack, I'm in awe. You're masterful in dealing with the older ladies."

"I meant every word of it, Abbie. You're like an ethereal angel in that gown. No woman at the ball compares because your beautiful heart glows in your face."

CHAPTER EIGHT

As she waited for Atwell to join her outside the Bonningtons' conservatory, to warm up her feet, Sabine stomped her flimsy boots on the frozen ground. She had a bad feeling about this whole evening, and the blasted falling snow was a sign. Finding and stealing the drawings out of the library during the holiday ball had been simple. Almost too simple, which just confirmed the rightness of the next move she was about to undertake in this dangerous dance of espionage.

Finally, Atwell showed up. "Sabine, is this really necessary? For God's sake, it's a bloody snowstorm."

"Yes, it is necessary." She didn't add, "to verify whether you've been double crossing the French."

She raised the lantern. "It's not far."

"I don't understand all this drama. Since we've got the plans, let's go before we're discovered. We can travel south to my estate and sail from Bournemouth."

Sabine was tired of repeating the same argument. Atwell had been insisting on them leaving immediately, before Bonnington discovered the missing documents, blind to the fact that this most likely was a ploy to trap them.

"Atwell, remember our plan was to study the drawings and return them. Also, it would be highly suspicious to leave the ball, let alone abandoning your wife there. It is much wiser for us to return to the ball and be seen departing separately. Not far from here there is a hut in the woods where we can study the drawings and then decide. Come along."

"Did Bonnington try to lure you to this hut, now that he's bored with his wife?"

How in blazes had Atwell had success in his embezzling scheme when he was so damn oblivious to everything around him? Because he was a bloody aristocrat who never paid attention to anything but himself. Bonnington was clearly smitten with his bride. He never left his bland, blond broodmare during the ball. That in itself made his drunken revelation to Atwell at the club all the more suspect. "No, I haven't spoken to him."

The cold air burned at her lungs making the short journey arduous. Gaston, her second in command, trailed behind them. He had already stridden the path, creating a green trail for her to follow.

Off the main path, the snow was deeper and wet slush seeped into her ankle boots, chilling her. The only sound in the subzero night was Atwell's heavy breathing from the exertion of walking a mere quarter of a mile, the falling snow muffling the song of the night birds and animal howls.

"How much farther? It is bloody cold."

Gaston, hired on by Bonnington's butler for the extra work required to host a ball, was the one who had discovered Bonnington's trysting spot. He had followed Bonnington and his wife to this secluded hut three days ago. The site was perfect for what she had in store for Atwell.

She kept her lantern low in her hand to avoid being sighted by the guards roaming the estate. Still, that made it difficult to see anything other than their feet. The silence and the shadows heightened the thrumming tension.

The trail ended in front of a sturdy wood hut. She expected a primitive shed, but the forester's hut appeared newly renovated with fresh wood and brickwork. Shaking the snow from her pelisse, she peered into the window before opening the heavy door.

A large bed was at the center of the space with a small table and chairs placed in front of the fireplace. Covered in red damask, with the cream linens and silk pillows, the bed was fit for the finest courtesan, not for an aristocratic arranged marriage. Opulent Persian rugs covered the floor and candles were spread throughout, giving the room an exotic and sensual air. She flashed on the memory of Bonnington's well-sculpted chest and lips and his predatory grin in their hours in bed. Sabine felt a twinge of something close to an emotion at the loss of Bonnington as a lover. She dismissed it quickly. Emotions were a luxury that she couldn't afford.

She placed the lantern on the small wood table, removing the silver candle holders.

"Spread the drawing on the table," Sabine directed Atwell. By his lascivious smirk, he registered the function of the hut's décor. "Surprising that Bonnington meets his mistress this close to his wife. He always seemed damn straitlaced."

Atwell dug into his waistcoat, bringing out the folded papers. Her freezing hands twitched at her side, eager to finish this business. She stood patiently waiting as Atwell smoothed the paper across the table.

Bending over the table, she evaluated the content. It was an architectural drawing, similar to the other drawings sent to them previously from Lieutenant Hyde.

Atwell bent his wide girth over to look closer as his finger traced the angles. "This is interesting. Bonnington made an X where he proposes to plant the explosive, but it is situated next to the entrance of the stairwell. That doesn't make sense. Why jeopardize the stairwell?"

Why indeed? They hadn't previously received any information about a stairwell for the Dover fortifications. Since Atwell had taken over as the mole, he had passed on information about the number of guns and men arriving at Dover. Nothing surprising or of any real significance had been in the information, the French military had expected the English to be fortifying one of the main ports to be invaded by the French ships.

Sabine continued the charade. "Stairwell to the tunnels? Sounds like a perfect place to blow up the French if they descend."

"The rationale for the stairwell is to move the troops quickly from the labyrinth of tunnels." With that one statement, Atwell revealed that he was withholding information on how the English planned to move troops at Dover. As she suspected, Atwell was being used to pass on misinformation. The English must have discovered his little embezzling game and recruited him. The plot was a trap for Atwell, as well as her.

It was time for her to act. If Bonnington and Rathbourne thought she had been fooled, they were underestimating her.

"Did you hear that noise?" Sabine whispered in a hushed tone.

Atwell's head jerked up. "I didn't hear anything. It's your nerves. You aren't used to all this intrigue."

"You're right. I'm not." She had trouble saying the words without laughing. "Can you look outside to make sure no one is coming?"

"Of course, my dear." Atwell walked the five steps to the door. There was irony all around for Atwell, a hapless dupe used by both sides.

With Gaston's pistol pointed at the center of his chest, Atwell backed into the hut. "What is the meaning of this?"

Seeing the cut on Gaston's lip and mussed clothing, Sabine asked. "Did you have a problem?"

"Your escort, Cosgrove, followed you."

"How exciting! Poor Captain Cosgrove. Did you kill him?"

"I didn't want to alert the guards with the sound of a gunshot until we're finished here. He's unconscious. Won't last long in these temperatures. We should be off."

"Sabine, you know this criminal?"

Yes, she knew Gaston in every way a woman knows a man. And after tonight's firestorm, she would need Gaston, the lusty youth, to unleash her excitement.

Gaston pressed the gun against Atwell's temple. "Take off your clothes and climb onto the bed."

Although the hut was frigid, sweat beaded on Atwell's forehead. "Is this a new way of punishing me, Sabine?"

Sabine couldn't suppress her hilarity. "Yes, Atwell. This is the ultimate punishment since you've been very bad. Now, take off your clothes."

Atwell looked between Gaston and Sabine, trying to gauge the situation.

"Now, you old fool." Gaston pulled the hammer back on the pistol.

Atwell unbuttoned his waistcoat quickly, aware of how unpredictable and deadly pistols could be. Atwell pulled on his cravat, his breathing loud as he eyed Gaston with licentious greed. "Sabine, you've outdone yourself." Atwell pulled down his breeches before removing his boots, his arousal indicating he was anticipating sex games with the well-built Gaston.

"Atwell, I should have brought Gaston sooner to entertain you. Where is the rope, Gaston?"

Atwell climbed onto the bed, giving them a clear view of his pasty, sagging arse. Sabine jerked her gaze away from the ghastly sight.

Gaston pointed next to the wood stove.

Their scheme was to make Atwell's death look like a night of bondage gone wrong. Lady Atwell would be notorious after her husband was found naked, strangled in his pursuit of pleasure on the Bonnington estate. A fitting end for Atwell and his arrogant wife, and a fitting wedding present from Sabine for the Bonningtons.

"Wait!" Gaston hissed and slipped behind the door.

The door opened slowly, giving Sabine time to pull out her pistol from underneath her dress.

Bonnington, pistol in hand, looked back and forth between Sabine with a rope in her hand and the nude, aroused Atwell on the bed. "Atwell, I don't remember giving you permission to use this place."

Sabine kept the pistol behind her back as she got into shooting range. "Is this a sacred bed since you take your wife here? Are you afraid a French whore might soil the sheets? Or do you dislike sharing your French whore?"

Sabine moved close enough to blow a hole in Bonnington with her small pistol. She didn't want to kill him, it would be a loss, but if Gaston couldn't subdue him…

Gaston raised his enormous, muscular arm and struck Bonnington with the butt of his pistol. Bonnington staggered, his gun swinging in a wild arc. Sabine raised her pistol. Gaston hit him again. The brutal blow had Bonnington staggering before falling to the floor, his eyes rolling back in his head.

"Sabine, was that necessary?" Atwell commanded from his propped position on the bed. "Now our evening is ruined. Bonnington is going to come after us."

Realizing that guards would come quickly, looking for the host of the party, Sabine pulled back the hammer and shot Atwell straight in the chest. He wasn't a difficult target. The shocked look on his face shot frissons of excitement through her. She would never tire of killing bloated aristocrats who believed they didn't bleed and die like their servants.

"Sabine?" He stared down at his chest, blood pouring onto the bedclothes.

"Throw Bonnington into the snow while I set this place on fire." It hadn't been part of her plan, but it seemed fitting to destroy Bonnington's love nest. She couldn't kill Bonnington, not because of any feelings. Rathbourne and his minions would be relentless in pursuing her if she killed him. Atwell didn't matter. He had outlived his usefulness for both sides.

"How far are the horses? We need to go."

Sabine opened the lid from the lantern and ignited Bonnington's drawing, then threw the flaming papers on the bed and waited to make sure the silk sheets caught fire before she slammed the door shut.

CHAPTER NINE

Lost in Jack's loving eyes and words, Abbie didn't notice Ford's approach. "Sir, Madam, I'm sorry to interrupt. It has come to my attention that Captain Cosgrove has disappeared."

Abbie's stomach plummeted. How could he be missing? Less than an hour ago, the attractive, rakish captain had been flirting with all the ladies, including Eliza, despite watching Sabine's movements in the crowded ballroom. The danger the agents faced suddenly became real.

"Disappeared?" Jack lowered his voice when he noticed his loud exclamation had drawn the attention of a group of guests standing nearby. "How could he disappear? Dewitt was assigned to follow him. Is he missing too?"

"No, Dewitt is in the hallway waiting for his orders. He trailed Cosgrove, at a distance, as instructed, on the path to Rathbourne Estate when suddenly Cosgrove vanished. To avoid exposure, neither man carried a lantern. Dewitt returned to ask whether you want to do a full search which might alert the suspects."

"Ford, you and I will search for Cosgrove. Tell Dewitt to remain at the door to the ballroom and guard Mrs. Bonnington. I'll join you at the conservatory door in five minutes."

Abbie tightly gripped Jack's arm while fear tightened its grip on her insides.

"Jack, shouldn't you take more men?"

"It is unfortunate timing that Brinsley had to go to London. And damn Rathbourne's instruction to keep our distance."

"If Sabine is as clever as we believe, she would have known if soldiers were shadowing her and Lord Atwell. Can't you take some of the men who are stationed around the house?"

"If we don't find Cosgrove, that is what I'll do. But before we tip off Sabine, Ford and I will search."

Setting a trap for Sabine was potentially dangerous. Abbie was alarmed at the thought of Jack being thrust into the midst of the peril. Chills of heat and cold fear chased over every inch of skin.

"Jack, promise me you'll be careful." Panic flashed through her with the memory of finding Jack, bleeding and unconscious after a brutal attack by a French spy. "I can't forget…"

"Darling, your hands are like ice." Jack pressed her thinly-gloved hands to his lips. "Don't worry. The last time I wasn't expecting to be attacked. This time, I'll be on my guard."

She didn't want to distract Jack with her need for reassurance. He had a job to do while her job was to remain in the ballroom and maintain the façade that all was normal to keep their guests unaware of the swirling intrigue.

"How will you find Cosgrove in the dark, snowy woods?"

"Most likely, Cosgrove turned off the path to follow Sabine and Atwell to the hut. That is the only thing that makes sense. Dewitt doesn't know about the hut. The only question is how did Atwell and Sabine know of the hut? It's our secret. She must have had men watching us. Abbie, you're not to leave the ballroom. Find Aunt Euphemia and stick close to her," Jack said in a severe tone.

"No one is interested in me. You're the one who needs to be careful, Jack." Abbie was pleased she had been able to maintain enough control of her emotions to prevent her voice from cracking. She was determined to remain calm for Jack's sake. She wouldn't want her husband interfering with her code-breaking work and she needed to respect his competence as a spy.

She made herself smile. "You promised me a dance. I'll be waiting."

"It won't take long at all. I'm sure I'll find Cosgrove by the hut. He and Ford will take Sabine into custody. And I will return to dance with my beautiful wife."

It was a logical deduction that Abbie usually would have appreciated, however, logic was inadequate when the heart was involved. For a scholar, this was painful to admit. Her heart beat frantically as she watched Jack head into imminent danger.

Abbie was boxed in on all sides, as most of London wanted to be acknowledged by the hostess. Courtesy demand that she speak to their many guests as she progressed through the crowd in search of Aunt Euphemia. Everything was a blur, as all she could think about was Jack.

Close to an hour had passed. Her desperation was growing by the minute, as was the urge to shove her guests out of the way and flee in search of Jack. She had to perform her assignment. She didn't have much farther before she made it to the entrance to the ballroom where, hopefully, she would find Dewitt and Aunt Euphemia.

"My darling girl, I've been looking for you." Abbie turned at the sound of Aunt Euphemia's voice. She was a stout woman of the same small stature as Abbie but appeared taller due to the large crimson turban festooned with holly leaves and berries she had donned.

"Aunt Euphemia, I must go look for Jack. He left over an hour ago, convinced that Captain Cosgrove had followed Sabine to a hut in the woods."

"I know, my dear. Dewitt informed me." She patted Abbie's arm.

Abbie waited for Aunt Euphemia to offer platitudes about worrying and remaining safely in the ballroom.

"I agree. Something is off. We need to investigate. Get your wrap and meet me at the conservatory door."

Terror seized her. "But the ball…"

"Mabel and Amelia are able to handle this group of people. And think of the great gossip with you, Jack, and Sabine all missing from the ball. Society will be entertained for weeks." Aunt Euphemia winked. "Be aware of anyone watching you, my dear. Haste is needed."

"Yes, of course." Suddenly Abbie could barely hear above the roaring pulse in her ears. Maintaining appearances vanished. Jack needed her.

Abbie was on high alert as she and Aunt Euphemia journeyed to the hut. She carried the lantern, lighting the way for the elderly woman, who was surprisingly spry on the uneven and slippery path.

She had many questions but remained silent, not wanting to disturb Aunt Euphemia's focus. If they were heading into danger, she needed to rely on Aunt Euphemia's skill. Abbie's forte was working in a library. Even so, Abbie could feel the tension radiating off the grand lady as her head swiveled back and forth, surveying the surroundings.

She wished she was with Jack, en route to their secret place in this winter wonderland of snow-laden yews and cedars and mighty oaks, instead of being frightened by what she and Aunt Euphemia might discover at the hut. Her sense of dread grew step by step. Jack had to be safe.

Abbie lifted the lantern for Aunt Euphemia to see the bend in the path, taking them downhill. "This is the first turn."

"Lower the lantern," Aunt Euphemia whispered. "And say nothing."

Abbie nodded, attempting to stifle her gnawing terror as they drew deeper into the woods. The eerie silence grew like a presence, filling the cold space. The sound of her rapid breathing was brash in the scary quiet.

Aunt Euphemia continued to lead the way. How could the older woman see?

When they came around the curve, an intense orange glow lit up the sky—massive flames were erupting from hut. Abbie gasped in desperation. "Oh, no. Please, God! Noooo."

Aunt Euphemia picked up her dress and ran ahead with Abbie following close by. Abbie need not tell her where to turn to the hut. The bright light and black billowing smoke against the dark sky were beacons. The acrid smoke burned Abbie's nose as the fire raged.

Abbie rushed behind Aunt Euphemia to the blazing hut. Horrified, Abbie stared, unable to speak.

A loud moan fractured the silence. Jack? Was her panic playing tricks on her?

Aunt Euphemia raised her hand for silence. She drew out a pistol and signaled Abbie to follow. Abbie's heart thrashed viciously against her chest as she followed Aunt Euphemia toward the sound.

She heard another moan coming from a snow drift just yards from the burning inferno. Abbie lifted her lantern to shine on the dark huddle while Aunt Euphemia aimed her pistol. Jack, her beautiful husband, covered in snow and ash, was trying to push himself upright. He collapsed backward with the effort.

Abbie rushed to him. "Oh, Jack. I've never been gladder to see you."

His face clenched in pain, he opened one eye. "Abbie?"

Abbie knelt in the snow to assess her injured husband. Blood stained the white snow where his head had lain. His face was pale, and he was panting.

He again attempted to push himself into a sitting position. "Help me up, Abbie. We need to find Cosgrove. Sabine is getting away."

He rubbed his hand along the back of the head. "I must have been hit with the butt of the gun. He has to be a big son of…to have hit me with such force."

Aunt Euphemia reappeared. "Bonnington, have you seen Cosgrove?"

Jack shook his head and then grabbed at his forehead, regretting the fast motion.

"No." Jack struggled to a sitting position.

"We'll get you back to the estate and call out the entire guard since Sabine has slipped through our net."

"Once I'm up, I can walk. We must find Cosgrove. Help me up, Abbie."

Abbie scrambled over a snow pile, her half boots sinking into the snow, to get a better position to support Jack's weight. She wrapped her arms around Jack from the back. Aunt Euphemia offered her hands to pull Jack forward out of the snow. Together, the two women, with assistance from Jack's mule-headed determination, got him upright. With the sudden jolt, he let out a ragged groan.

His body shuddered as he swayed, almost falling backward if it hadn't been for Abbie's tight grip on his waist.

Jack's drive to remain standing in spite of his injury was impressive, reflecting his strong will and powerful constitution.

"I should tend to the gash on the back of your head." Abbie leaned forward to examine the large gash.

"The icy snow stopped the bleeding. Once we find Cosgrove, you can attend to me all night." Jack's usual rakish swagger would have been effective if he hadn't staggered when he tried to wiggle his eyebrows.

Aunt Euphemia marched ahead of them with her gun pointed ahead. Her vigilance kept Abbie on guard, dispelling any notion that they were out of danger. Threats lurked around every corner.

Usually, Jack's body was as heated as a blasting fireplace. Not now. He was frigid from the cold. He could have died from exposure, let alone the head wound, if she and Aunt Euphemia hadn't found him.

Her body started to tremble with the shock. A strange mix of alarm and rage took over her body as the what-ifs played through her brain in slow and vivid agony. She wanted to shout at her husband for risking his life.

"Aunt Euphemia, take Abbie home. I'm going to follow the tracks that lead away from the hut."

The air was so crisp that it hurt her lungs to breathe. That didn't prevent her from yelling at her injured husband. "What is going through your pig-headed brain? You can't go by yourself with a major wound!" Her fears powered her shout.

Aunt Euphemia raised her hand in warning and then pressed a finger to her lips to signal silence as they approached the main path back to the Bonnington estate.

Hugging Jack closer to prevent him from falling and to warm him, Abbie halted, waiting for instructions from Aunt Euphemia.

"Sabine, I won't hesitate to shoot you after what your man did to me." Captain Cosgrove's distinctive baritone echoed in the woods. "And if you think I'm angry, just wait until Bonnington sees his hut."

"Cosgrove, you're a fool." Sabine replied with her distinctive throaty laugh.

Jack gestured to Aunt Euphemia, who took Abbie's arm with one hand and pulled her behind a tree—her other hand steady on her small pistol

Jack, who seconds before was unsteady on his feet, stood bolt upright and waited to be discovered.

"Well, isn't this a touching moment. Sabine, you've been a very bad girl."

Abbie had to cover her mouth to keep from shouting again at Jack. Why was he taunting the evil woman? My heavens. She had married an impossible, really impossible, man.

"Jack, *mon cherie*, are you upset by my handiwork? And Lady Bonnington, you can come out from behind the tree. Your bright blue pelisse is quite obvious. What a pathetic creature. Hiding behind a tree, allowing an old woman to protect you." Sabine stepped toward Jack. "You find that kind of woman alluring?"

Abbie's rage combusted. How dare she? Abbie stepped out from her hiding place, ignoring Aunt Euphemia's hiss before she trailed Abbie onto the path. Her gun never wavered and now was pointed at Sabine.

"Abbie, get back. She is baiting you in her game."

Did anyone here realize she wasn't a fool or some sort of insipid creature? She understood Sabine's purpose. It was basic distract-and-divert your attention away from your main purpose. And it was the reason Abbie stepped out—to protect Jack. The main reason for this dramatic scene, engineered by a desperate Sabine, was to harm her husband. Abbie understood Jack's red-haired temper and his need to defend his wife made him vulnerable to Sabine's machinations.

"Sabine, here I am. Not hiding." As she stepped into the clearing, Abbie's heart slammed against her chest, reckless, erratic, and wild.

Jack grabbed her arm and tried to push her behind him when Sabine bent down. And then chaos reigned. Aunt Euphemia stepped in front of Abbie to block her from the knife that Sabine had pulled from beneath her dress. Jack fired his pistol as Captain Cosgrove leaped to tackle Sabine. Jack's shot was true, hitting Sabine in the chest, right where her heart should have been.

Sabine crumpled onto the ground, her blood saturating the snow.

EPILOGUE

It was Christmas, a day to celebrate love and hope. And, despite last night's "events," Abbie refused to allow French spies and ex-mistresses to ruin her first Christmas with her husband.

Their houseguests had departed. Now, before the family's Christmas dinner, exchange of presents, and church services, Abbie wanted to slip away with her husband. She had something very important to share.

However, Jack was nowhere to be found. She had heard his voice in the hallway after he organized sledding for his exuberant brothers before tonight's celebrations. Eliza, not in the least tired from her first ball, had gone with the boys and the assortment of dogs. And hearing of Eliza's participation, Captain Cosgrove had decided to join the fun. Abbie needed to talk with Jack about the captain's interest in her younger sister. Eliza, an innocent country girl, was no match for the sophisticated rake who, according to Jack, ran in the same jaded circles her husband had before joining the military.

Abbie paced the main hallway, anxious for Jack's return, not wanting to interrupt Aunt Euphemia's conversation in the drawing room with Jack's father. They were engaged in a heated discussion about women's sidesaddles. Hotchkiss reported that Jack had gone outdoors, expecting to return within a half hour.

The only logical explanation was that he had slipped off to speak with Lord Rathbourne. Since Captain Cosgrove had reported everything last night so Jack and Abbie could return to the holiday ball and their guests as if nothing unseemly occurred, Jack's discussion with Rathbourne shouldn't last long, Abbie rationalized.

Abbie had never realized that she had hidden talents of subterfuge as she and Jack concocted a wild story to explain their absence from the ball. Jack had related to their guests that he and Abbie had gone in search of Colin and Drew, who had gone outside to play in the snow and had gotten lost in the woods because of the snowstorm. Jack's gash was explained away as an incidental bump from a low-hanging tree branch. The guests moved quickly onto the more scintillating gossip of the unexplained disappearance of Lord Atwell and Sabine.

Abbie heard Jack's voice at the front door. She hurried along the corridor to catch her husband before he could be waylaid by anyone.

Jack inspected Abbie from boots to her wool pelisse and ermine muff and scarf. "Abbie, how did you know that I wanted to take you outside?"

"You do?"

Did he already know what she had in mind? She had told no one. "I wanted to take you outside too."

"I guess that's settled." A wolfish grin lit up Jack's face. "May I?" Jack offered his arm to escort Abbie out the door into the sunny, sparkling Christmas Day.

Descending the steps that had been cleared of last night's snowfall, Jack bent and brushed his soft lips along Abbie's. "Merry Christmas, Mrs. Bonnington."

"Merry Christmas, my dear husband." Abbie, touched her hand to Jack's face, loving the morning bristle along his chin. "How is your headache? Did you take another headache powder?"

"I did take one this morning. If the French keep bashing me on the head, I'm going to have a permanent dent. Will you still love me?"

"Don't make jokes, Jack, please." Abbie gazed into her husband's violet eyes, noting the shadows under his eyes from the pain he was masking. "I have something to say to you and I want to do it at our 'special place.'"

Abbie took Jack's hand and laced it with hers inside her muff. "Let's walk there before we have to return for the festivities."

"Darling, are you sure you're ready to return to the woods?"

"I'm sure. I want to go to our place." The path glistening in the sunlight was beautiful and clean, not anything like last night's dark and threatening woods. The day was fresh and new nature's way of expunging the darkness. The hopefulness of the season sang in Abbie's heart.

They would break up the French spy ring operating in London. Captain Cosgrove had discovered Sabine's diary when he had rushed to her townhouse before the French discovered her demise. By deciphering the diary's code, Abbie was hopeful they would identify the French spymaster.

"There is nothing there. I had men clear the area."

Abbie was glad that Jack didn't mention removing Lord Atwell's remains. Abby shuddered at the memory of Lady Atwell's bewildered face as she was escorted home by Sergeant Dewitt last evening. Jack had reassured Abbie that Rathbourne would spare Lady Atwell the details of her husband's death.

"You're shivering. Maybe this isn't a great idea to return to the place where you suffered a trauma."

Abbie tugged on Jack's hand. "We have to reclaim our place. And today, Christmas Day is the day."

"If you'd like, I thought we could rebuild a hut on the other side of the estate away from the memories of last night." Her husband's voice softened.

"I want to rebuild on our spot. It belongs to us. A monument to love. With the war ahead, we must not give in to despair. Not on Christmas Day, a day of hope. I want love to win out, not evil and hate."

Jack pulled Abbie into his arms. "I love you Abbie. I love your strength and your courage. And when the weather permits, we'll start rebuilding."

"I love you, Jack."

Abbie nestled closer to Jack to gather his heat, glad to draw in his warmth and glad for his return to health. The smell of smoke still lingered in the woods. It was important for her to say what was in her heart on Christmas.

Abbie halted where the hut used to stand. Beyond ashes and fragments of wood, nothing remained except the brick chimney and the wood stove. Abbie stared at the stove, her eyes not believing what she was seeing. Smoke was coming out of the wood stove.

"Jack, is that a fire in the wood stove? Who would light a fire?"

"I did, hoping to bring you here."

"How did you know that I'd be willing to come?"

"I didn't. However, it seems you and I had the same thought. Our next hut will be a phoenix rising out of the ashes. I wasn't willing to have Sabine and her evil manipulations take away our place of great joy. I came to light the fire in hopes of enticing you to light a metaphorical candle, never guessing that you would have the same idea."

Abbie wrapped her arms around Jack. "How did I get such a brilliant husband?"

"I don't feel I deserve you, my brilliant code breaker."

"I want to tell you today, on this day of hope and love, how important you are to me. During the time you were missing, I was terrified that I might lose you and I resolved to tell you. I've been impatient and resistant to your need to guard me, but now I understand. I understand your words of 'loving me like a crazy person.' That's exactly how I feel, Jack."

She brushed away the tears. "I'm not sure I can let you go after Gaston with Captain Cosgrove tomorrow. The logical part of my brain argues that you must go and we must fight for our country. As your wife who needs you and loves you, I want to have you stay home, stay safe, and do the estate business. But you would never be happy without doing your part, and I couldn't be happy if you weren't."

"Abbie, darling. Let's us vow, on this our first Christmas, to love each other like crazy people for the rest of our lives, no matter what is going on in the world."

The End

Enjoy an excerpt from

A Code of Honor

The Code Breakers Series, Book 6

BY

JACKI DELECKI

CHAPTER ONE

The Honorable John Andrew Bonnington, following the shrieks of laughter and barking, bolted over the fence, too impatient to walk to the gate connecting the family's St. John's Wood estate and his sister's newly acquired estate.

His younger brothers and their best buddy, Edward Harcourt, had disappeared into the bright March sunshine for a cricket match. Most likely with their cricket-fanatic older sister.

He could have sent their tutor to fetch the wayward brothers, but the bright weather was the perfect excuse to leave the forlorn empty house. Like his younger brothers, Jack also felt the absence of his newlywed sister.

By the loud barking and yipping, Wellesley, the family's Labrador puppy, Matilda and Mirabelle, the spaniels, and Gus, Edward's constant Labrador companion were also enjoying their liberation from the confines of the house.

Hearing Drew's boisterous laugh, Jack snapped out of his frustration with his unruly siblings. Amelia was keenly missed by the thirteen-year-old boy. Amelia had been a surrogate mother since their mother died in birthing Drew.

Coming down the steep incline, Jack expected to see his sister's flaming red hair and long stride running in the open field. Instead, he was shocked to see the boys huddled around a young woman lying flat on the cold spring ground.

Edward swung the cricket bat in one hand while Colin leaned over the tiny blond woman. The dogs circled the prostrate form and yipped playfully. What had the boys done this time? Knocked the lady unconscious?

He ran. His heart pounding making it difficult to hear what Colin was saying to the fallen lady.

"I assumed you'd know that you can't stand on the home base," Colin apologized.

Edward shoved Colin. "How would she know since she's never played before?"

Then Jack heard a light, lyrical laugh. "No harm except for my pride. I hadn't thought that you would so easily knock me off my feet. I've always wished to be taller."

Jack's voice thundered as he increased his gait. "What have you done this time, Colin?"

The boys separated to give him a clear view of the lady. And there, in dishabille, was his nemesis, Miss Abigail Lyon. The maddening woman smiled up at him as if nothing was amiss. Her bandeau, supposedly holding her riotous curls in place, covered one eye, and her bright curls fell around her shoulders in wanton disarray as if she had recently been tumbled.

Jack pushed his brother aside to lift Miss Lyon off the cold, wet ground. "Are you injured?"

"No. I'm quite fine." She was a tiny thing and light as a bird, unlike his gangly sister. His body hardened immediately by the way her soft curves pressed against him.

"My brothers knocked you down?"

"The boys have been everything a lady would want in gentlemanly behavior." Her voice was laced with amusement. Her bright blue eyes were wide and close enough to see the gold striations like streaks of sunlight in the cornflower blue.

"You definitely have sustained a head injury if you are calling these ruffians gentlemen." Jack couldn't look away from her shining face. "Have you any injuries?"

She was close enough to see that her lower lip was wider than her top and looked pillow soft and perfect for... He jerked his eyes away.

Despite her reddening face, she pushed against his chest with a puny effort. "I'm in no need of an unwanted rescue. Put me down."

Colin interrupted. "I'm really sorry, Abbie."

Jack twisted to give his brother his best polite-company stare of "what the hell are you doing."

"Colin, you forget yourself. 'Miss Lyon' to you."

The soft bundle of woman wrestled against him. "I've given the boys permission to call me Abbie."

Jack was enjoying her tiny and futile attempts to release herself. She was like the puppy, Wellesley, with her uncoordinated efforts. His thoughts veered to how he would stop her from struggling with a warm kiss if she were another woman and if his brothers and Edward weren't watching in rapt attention.

"You can unhand me. I'm not some damsel in distress. Besides, you're interrupting our game and my team is winning." She twisted in his arms, brushing his chest again with her abundant breasts. She wasn't tiny in the areas that mattered most to men. "Isn't that right, Drew?"

He reminded himself what a frustrating piece of baggage Miss Abigail Lyon was. His expanding and tightening male body didn't seem to care as he lowered 'Abbie' to the ground. He needed to get to his townhouse and his gentlemanly pursuits if a hoyden could give an immediate and out of control physical reaction.

She whacked at her skirt to loosen the wet grass from the shiny material.

An animated Drew pulled on Jack's arm. "Jack, Amelia, Abbie, and I are beating Colin and Edward." Being the younger brother and the tag-along to Colin and Edward wasn't always easy for the usually sunny boy.

With Drew's enthusiasm, all the dogs started yelping again. Wellesley jumped on Drew's leg despite Jack's constant admonition not to allow the dog to jump. Weeks ago, feeling helpless about how to help his brother with Amelia's marriage, Jack had decided to get Drew a puppy. Not his best idea since Wellesley was chewing everything in his path, adding to the burden of the already overwhelmed staff left to the care of two rambunctious youths.

Jack looked between the young faces. "Where is our tomboy of a sister?"

He ignored Abbie's gasp.

Drew kicked at the grass with the toe of his boot. "Brinsley just arrived home from a trip, and Amelia acted like he had been away for a year. She got all gushy. Brinsley asked to speak to her inside. What could he be saying that's taking this long?"

Abbie stared wide-eyed at Jack, her lips turned up in amusement.

"Brinsley, knowing how much Amelia loves cricket, shouldn't be interrupting the game," Drew added.

Colin and Edward remained silent.

Jack didn't know if Colin had any idea of why Brinsley had detained Amelia, Jack certainly did, but he didn't want to imagine his sister and Brinsley together.

"It must be very important for Amelia to give up a game of cricket," Drew pouted.

Abbie's snort had all the boys turning toward her.

"What's so amusing?" Edward had the keen intellect of his older siblings. "Amelia is one of the best cricket players. She'd rather play cricket than almost anything else."

"She does like fashion design and painting," Colin added.

Jack mentally shut down that his sister's newest passion might replace cricket.

"Abbie's been a good sport despite not knowing the game." Admiration reflected in Colin's violet eyes that matched his own.

He could understand Colin's fascination with Abbie's shining eyes and her enthusiastic manner with no artifice. Until she opened her mouth, revealing her irritating address. He need not socialize with the irritating Miss Lyon since he'd only be staying with the boys for a few weeks to help them settle into their new routine. If he wanted drama, he could go to town and renew his relationship with Sabine.

He barked. "And what of your lessons? I come home to find Mr. Merriman and the household searching for you."

The simultaneous moans had no effect on Jack. Mr. Merriman had been Jack's tutor and he remained grateful to the scholar for the intellectual discipline he had instilled, despite all of Jack's ploys to avoid studying.

"You're not at all like Amelia. She wouldn't make us study on a day like today. Today is the first day we can be outside after all the rain. I'm not going home. I want Amelia. She promised us tea."

"Mutiny, is it my laddie?" Jack lifted his younger brother, turning him upside down and dangling him by his feet. Jack turned toward Colin and Edward. "What do you say? Make him walk the plank?"

Jack lowered Drew closer to his puppy who was jumping to lick Drew's face. Drew burst into laughter. "Or are kisses from Wellesley enough punishment?"

Pandemonium broke out when Colin and Edward shouted "Plank. Plank." The other dogs rushed to be part of the game and circled Drew barking, ready to pounce.

Jack dangled Drew one last time before throwing him over his shoulder. "Matey, I think it's the plank for you."

Although Colin and Edward were too old to play pirates, the idea of the plank which involved jumping off their father's library table still provided entertainment.

Jack placed Drew on his feet. "We need to inform Mr. Merriman and the staff where you've been. And we'll have tea at home."

"We can't leave. Amelia hasn't come out to finish the game." Drew's eyes, so much like their mother's, made Jack immediately want to soothe the boy's feelings. Jack was fifteen when he lost his sunny and affectionate mother. He didn't want Drew to suffer by the loss of Amelia as he had by the loss of his mother.

Abbie leaned over Drew. "Let's resume our game tomorrow. I'm sure there is time in your schedule to play. I'm not clear on why your brother is being a stickler for studies since he doesn't actually see a benefit in higher learning."

Abbie's chin thrust out as if daring him to argue. "Oh, my faulty memory." She tapped her finger on the plump lower lip. "He just doesn't believe there's a benefit for women."

Jack stifled all the swear words forming on his lips when Drew tugged on Abbie's arm. "You promise you and Amelia will play tomorrow?"

"I can't promise for Amelia, but I will definitely be available."

He didn't need the little baggage interfering with the boy's schedule. "And how long will we have the pleasure of your company in the neighborhood, Miss Lyon?"

"It's great news, Jack. Abbie is staying with Amelia until the Season starts." Colin beamed at Abbie. "It will give us plenty of time to teach you cricket."

Abbie curtsied to the boys. "Thank you, kind gentlemen, for your open-mindedness in my ability to learn." She raised her eyebrows at Jack, baiting him to respond. He wasn't going to debate again with Miss Abigail Lyon whether women should be able to attend university.

"Since my sister and her husband are departing for Scotland, Amelia has asked me to stay with her until my family arrives in town for the Season."

"That is thoughtful of Amelia." His sister was either matchmaking or seeking revenge by forcing him to interact with Miss Lyon after all the times he and Parker, the next oldest brother, tortured Amelia. Unlike brothers who settled disputes with pummeling each other, sisters were very crafty. Ever since Miss Lyon and he had butted heads over a woman's right to study at university, Amelia got that fiery gleam in her eye when they were together. She'd enjoying seeing his loss of droll indifferent manner, one he had mastered at the finest drawing rooms.

"I'm surprised my sister needs more company since she has a new husband." His rude words smothered the defiance and winning gleam out of Miss Lyon.

She adjusted the bandeau on her head. "Brinsley has more trips planned, and Amelia is in need of female company."

Jack had heard rumors about Brinsley having a French mistress. But he refused to believe the man would betray his spirited sister. Brinsley's reputation before he married Amelia had been unsavory. His rumored elopement to his brother's fiancée had been untrue. In fact, Brinsley had saved Miss Lyon's elder sister from marrying his violent brother. If Brinsley thought he could get away with hurting Amelia, Jack would take his brother-in-law on, despite his imposing size and reputation as a brawler.

Drew shifted from one foot to the other before lifting his puppy into his arms. "Amelia promised us food. Aren't you getting hungry, Wellesley?"

Gus, Edward's rotund yellow Lab, infamous for stealing food off tea trays, barked in answer to Drew's query.

Everyone laughed. And Abbie's bright eyes gleamed in appreciation. She bent to pat Gus. "You're hungry too, Gus?"

Colin gestured toward the Brinsley's newly-purchased estate. "We don't have to go home. Betsy will feed us."

Amelia had appointed her maid to be the housekeeper of her new home. The boys and Betsy had grown up together.

"We need to go home. I'm sure I can convince Mrs. Wells to include last night's shepherd's pie for a snack."

"Shepherd's pie?" Edward, like Colin, was at the age of constant eating. "And her biscuits?"

Drew looked up at Abbie. "It isn't the same without Amelia. Colin grabs all the food before I can get my share. If you come, Colin and Edward will have to behave."

"I'm not sure Miss Lyon wants to be subjected to you ruffians after the damage she sustained at the cricket field."

Jack shared a glance at the woman. He was trying to spare her his high-spirited brothers and the chaos that regularly erupted at teatime at Bonnington house.

"Thank you, sir, for considering my delicate feelings. But I have one younger brother and four younger sisters and am quite able to preside over teatime."

Colin turned to Edward. "Race you to the house for the first biscuits."

"That's not fair. You're taller than I am," Drew shouted at the two racing boys. "You can't start tea without Abbie."

Jack didn't have to worry yet about Colin's infatuation with Abbie since food seemed still to be the priority, but the day would come. Jack didn't want to consider it.

Jack offered his arm to Abbie. He shouldn't be calling her Abbie in his mind.

"I will remind you that teatime with the Bonningtons isn't worth risking your life over. I did warn you."

CHAPTER TWO

Abbie took a dainty bite of the biscuit, careful not to drop any morsels on her lap. She then patted her lips with a napkin confirming that no crumbs remained on her lips. All her careful requirements of a lady were lost on her companions who stuffed food into their mouths, barely pausing to chew before reaching again to pile their plates.

Her mother would have a conniption if she witnessed today's tea at Bonnington Estate. After she had fainted at the news that Abbie was unchaperoned in the company of four gentlemen and four dogs, all of whom were focused more on the shepherd's pie, biscuits, and the ham than her virtue. Of course, the so-called gentlemen were under the age of sixteen except for one and they were more interested in the cheese and buttered bread than proper decorum.

She snuck glances at Mr. Bonnington from under her eyelashes. His long legs, encased in tight riding breeches, stretched out in front of him. She tried to maintain her ladylike disinterest in his ungentlemanly behavior of not sitting upright. By his lazing posture and indifferent manner, he clearly demonstrated that he didn't know how to conduct himself in polite Society.

Not that she had much experience with gentleman's behavior or polite Society. Since the rumor of her sister Lauren's scandalous elopement with Lord Brinsley, their family remained at their estate with few visitors. Only Lord Brinsley's respectable marriage to the most esteemed Miss Amelia Bonnington qualified the Lyon family's acceptance to rejoin good Society.

The truth that Lauren had been taken to Scotland to teach in a girl's school rather than scandalously eloping with Lord Brinsley had finally been accepted. Now, allowed back into the fold of polite Society, Abbie, at the ancient age of twenty-two, was to be paraded this Season like a prized sow at the market for a proper match. Her father hadn't learned from his attempt at selling his first daughter for land and title to the violent Marquis of Falconbridge. Abbie was to make an advantageous marriage and secure the future and happiness of her four younger sisters as her mother reminded her daily.

Resentment burned through her. No one considered or cared what she desired or planned for her future.

"Have our so-called gentlemanly manners ruined your appetite?" Mr. Bonnington's eyebrows raised in haughty condescension.

Unaware of the company, she had been holding her cup in mid-air, lost in her dire thoughts—an unpardonable offense in her mother's estimation.

Abbie placed her cup in the saucer. Ignoring the need to counter that her standards for the boys' behavior didn't apply to adult gentlemen who broke the cardinal rule by mentioning a woman's appetite. Her mother had also been clear that you never discussed anything to do with bodily functions in the presence of a lady—no slouching, no chewing with open mouths, and no conversation that would surely upset anyone's digestion.

"If I remember correctly, you did say…" Mr. Bonnington gestured toward his brothers and Edward with only one arm since the other held bread piled with cheese and ham. "They were gentlemen."

Not that she'd ever admit to the conceited man that she knew little about boys or young men. "I'm not accustomed to the volume of food boys require. My brother is still in the nursery."

"It's too bad Parker isn't here. He can eat more than any of us." Colin laughed, around the ham in his mouth. Abbie envisioned her mother's pinched lips if she witnessed Colin's mortal sin of speaking with food in his mouth. It would be rather amusing to witness her mother's reaction. She'd probably need to take to her bed for days which always was a reason for celebration for the Lyon sisters. "But he's off to fight Bonny. I wish I were old enough to join the fight."

"Well, I for one, am glad Parker's not here," Edward said. "We'd have to eat faster."

Amelia gaped. This was eating slowly?

Mr. Bonnington grinned.

Abbie couldn't look away. How dashing he became when he smiled—the little crinkles around his bright violet eyes, the same striking shade as Amelia. She could understand why he was a favorite with the ladies. All ladies wanted to reform rakes. Supposedly, in polite Society, countenance and charm were regarded as the highest attributes—higher than a man's thinking and principles. And, since women weren't considered capable of forming their own opinions, a woman was only measured by her countenance and charm. Abbie had no desire to develop those qualities further.

"For the Bonnington boys, this is a civilized tea. It's also the reason we don't have visitors. And I did warn you." He spoke in the same supercilious, cringe-worthy tone as her mother.

Of course, he needed to point out that he had been right. His eyes gleamed in satisfaction, once he expressed his superior knowledge. Despite the way the sunlight shone on his mahogany hair, making him seem sharp and strong, a lady with only half a brain would immediately recognize the extent of his prideful pig-headedness.

Ignoring Mr. Bonnington, Abbie leaned forward and reached for the teapot. "Does anyone's tea need refreshing?"

"Thank you, Abbie." Colin smiled, lifting his cup for her to serve him. His eyes were darker than his brother's but soon Colin's mischievous smile would charm all the ladies.

"I tried to talk my father into allowing me to join the cavalry. Richard, our son's gardener, is only one year older than I am and he enlisted. Father went apoplectic, threatened to send me to Eton."

Abbie stared at Colin, the teapot in mid-air. "You want to join the army?" Her mind grasping at this foreign world and this foreign conversation.

"Of course! We can't sit around and wait for Napoleon to invade England. We have to attack him first."

This conversation wasn't fit for ladies. Abbie's spirits soared with the possibility of a non-censored discussion.

"He'll attack Dover." Colin cut a wedge from the Stilton cheese. "Don't you agree, Jack?"

"But since we'll be expecting the Dover invasion and preparing for it, I believe Napoleon, who is a brilliant strategist, might not attack Dover," Mr. Bonnington said. The Straits of Dover were the shortest stretch of Channel separating Britain from the Continent and was therefore of immense strategic value through the centuries. Abbie might have never discussed war strategies but she read history books. She surreptitiously read everything in her father's library.

"That is the challenge: how to anticipate the invasion based on his previous strategies," Edward added before chomping loudly on an apple slice.

"Parker told us that more troops will be deployed to Ireland in case Napoleon tries again to invade from the North," Colin added. "Everyone expects he will also attempt a water invasion."

"He's been recruiting the Irish for years attempting to capitalize on their antipathy toward us," Mr. Bonnington said.

"Hold your friends close but your enemies closer," Colin bellowed in an imperious voice.

Drew laughed loudly. "Crikey. That sounds just like Merriman."

Hiding her shock and fascination that the boys could quote Machiavelli and discuss battle strategies was difficult, especially since Mr. Bonnington watched her very closely. She didn't care that she couldn't hide her interest in this heady and interesting discussion. Teatime at the Lyon household was a time for lessons on social deportment. After the scandal, her mother repeated endlessly while she whimpered into her handkerchief that if they were ever allowed again in good company, the Lyon sisters would be held to higher standards than other ladies.

"The Royal Navy will stop him." Drew took a big gulp of tea. "We've ruled the high seas since Queen Elizabeth."

"Yes, but Dover has to be fortified in case he does succeed in making land," Edward added. "I'm sure the plans are underway. The difficulty is forecasting the invasion."

"Might they not predict the invasion by the tide charts? And the weather will have to be considered since it will affect the speed of the vessels." Abbie blurted this out before she could temper her excitement at joining such a discussion.

"The admiralty is well aware that they must follow the tides to predict," Colin added. "The greater difficulty is in predicting the weather."

"You could increase the predictions by devising a mathematical model if there was a way to look at the previous storms and tides." Abbie's mind was spinning on how she would devise such an algorithm. She stared into space, another habit which her mother hated, while her mind churned with mathematical formulas.

Abbie looked up to find Mr. Bonnington examining her face carefully.

Oh fiddlesticks, now she had done it. She took a sip of her cold tea, avoiding his intense scrutiny.

"The Admiralty has all the information. And I'm sure the East India Company, as well as the insurance companies, keep records of the sailing tides as well as past storms since they have to pay out when a ship and its merchandise are lost," Mr. Bonnington added.

Now embarrassed by her ignorance of how commerce and the male-dominated world worked, she busied herself adjusting the napkin on her lap. She knew nothing of the East India trading company and its commerce.

"What about the invasion by air balloons? I'd like a chance to shoot one of those down." Drew pointed a pretend gun into the air to blast the balloon from the sky.

"That is why Dover has to be fortified with cannons to shoot down the air balloons before they land."

Edward chomped on another apple slice.

"Air balloons?" Abbie couldn't hide her keen interest. "French soldiers arriving by air. How fascinating."

"You don't know about the air balloons?" Drew's mouth hung open. "Everyone knows about them."

The boys all looked up to stare at her as if she were a

three-legged cow. The shock on the boys' faces reflected on how limited her experience of the world. Here she was, older than anyone of them and knew nothing about Napoleon's plan. Her knowledge of the world was based on the books she smuggled out of her father's library.

"Ladies aren't allowed to fill their minds with such frightening ideas. It is our gentlemanly duty to protect them from worries by not exposing them to the reality of the world," Mr. Bonnington intoned.

Abbie felt the flush of anger starting at her toes and working its way to her face and ready to blast out of her mouth. Of all the twaddle.

Mr. Bonnington grinned, waiting for her retort. Why did she get the feeling the man was baiting her?

Enjoy an excerpt from

Men Under

FIRE

Book Three in the Grayce Walters Romantic Suspense Series

BY

JACKI DELECKI

CHAPTER ONE

Sergeant Nick Welby forced himself to look up at the plane roaring above him and ignore his primitive instinct to break into a run. His heart punched against his chest in painful thuds. A Boeing 737—not enemy fire. Seattle's Fremont neighborhood—not Afghanistan.

He took a calming breath and then another. The hipster neighborhood, filled with buzzing cars and rushing crowds, ratcheted his already revved-up nervous system, making every sound and movement chafe against his jangled nerves like an open wound.

Talley, Nick's military partner, a bomb-sniffing canine, strained against her lead.

The golden lab, like him, was tense and hyper-alert, waiting for disaster to strike. Both he and his dog were on sick leave. A month had helped to heal their physical injuries, but neither had made progress in calming their stress reactions. They both saw and felt danger everywhere every day.

He stared up at the refurbished warehouse situated on the waterway to Puget Sound. Adrenaline surged through his body at the idea of walking into the unknown building. He was sweating heavily, as if he were still in the heat of the

Registan desert instead of the August summer day in the Northwest.

A white-and-black sign hung on the warehouse: *Grayce Walters, DVM, Animal Acupuncturist.* He bent and petted the attentive dog. Talley's soft chocolate eyes echoed the feelings stuck in his throat. "I don't like it any better than you do, but this doctor will help you."

Nick didn't have a lot of hope for his own recovery, but he couldn't let his partner suffer. Doc Samson, the Welby family's veterinarian, had sworn by the amazing skill of this doctor. He paused and blew the air out of his constricted lungs and then pulled the door open. He'd do anything to help his partner heal from the IED explosion that had almost taken both their lives, even walk into this dangerous unknown.

———

Nick's mind and body were at ease after the hour with Dr. Walters. Doc Samson was right-on—the tiny woman had special gifts. Having been raised on a horse farm, Nick had immediately recognized the veterinarian's intuitive connection in relating to and comforting animals.

Simply being in Dr. Walters's presence was restorative, as evidenced by Talley sleeping soundly on the floor. As Talley's handler, he was connected to the dog at a level most people couldn't understand. When his partner relaxed, he felt the same.

Dr. Walters, looked up from her note taking. "I'd like to treat Talley once a week for the next three months. You live in Auburn. Will it be a problem to drive into Seattle?"

"Not a problem, ma'am. I'd do anything for this dog."

She leaned across her desk. "Do you swim, sergeant?"

"Yes, ma'am." He didn't have a clue what swimming had to do with the acupuncture.

"I'd like you and Talley to start swimming in a lake or deep river. It's important you do it together."

"Lake Youngs is close by our family farm. Talley and I can swim there."

"Water will soothe Talley's ratcheted up nervous system."

Why did he feel as if the doctor wasn't talking just about Talley?

She closed the file on her desk. "Don't do any training around the swimming. Talley needs a real break from her work. Her senses, especially her focus and her nose are working overtime. She'll have a break in the water."

Nick nodded. "It'll be great to swim after our morning runs."

"Sounds like we've got a plan. Let's see how the swimming works." Dr. Walters stood from her desk and walked toward the door. "I can hear that my assistant is back. She'll make your appointment for next week."

Talley sat up with the doctor's movements. With her front paws planted forward, the usually hyper dog stretched her spine and then slowly hoisted herself to follow Dr. Walters. He couldn't explain exactly what had happened, but like Talley, he felt a deep sense of relaxation. For the first time since he had arrived stateside, he could breathe calmly and catch glimpses of the contented man before the war. He and a tranquil Talley followed the doctor to the outer office.

Dr. Walters stopped suddenly in the doorway. A young, curvaceous woman was balanced on the stool, reaching into cupboards, as she sang the painful lyrics from Nirvana's song "Sliver."

When she stretched her entire body forward, her short black skirt inched higher, giving him an incredible view of her sweet, rounded backside. He swore under his breath at the tempting sight. She wore fishnet tights and thigh-high boots that were right out of every red-blooded male's fantasy.

His whole body tightened, not in danger but in hunger. Lust and need hummed through him, an invigorating feeling that he hadn't experienced in a very long time.

ABOUT THE AUTHOR

Jacki Delecki is a best-selling romantic suspense author. Delecki's contemporary Grayce Walters Series, which chronicles the adventures of a Seattle animal acupuncturist, was an editor's selection by *USA Today*. Delecki's Regency series, The Code Breakers, hit number one on Amazon.

To learn more about Jacki and her books and to be the first to hear about contests and giveaways join her newsletter found on her website: www.JackiDelecki.com. Follow her on FB—JDelecki; Twitter @jackidelecki; BookBub—jacki-delecki; Goodreads—Jacki_Delecki; and Amazon—Jacki-Delecki.

www.ingramcontent.com/pod-product-compliance
Lightning Source LLC
Chambersburg PA
CBHW071009120726
47910CB00004B/1445